HARRIET TUBMAN: LIVE IN CONCERT

HARRIET TUBMAN: LIVE IN CONCERT

A NOVEL

BOB THE
DRAG QUEEN

G

GALLERY BOOKS

New York   Amsterdam/Antwerp   London
Toronto   Sydney/Melbourne   New Delhi

G

Gallery Books
An Imprint of Simon & Schuster, LLC
1230 Avenue of the Americas
New York, NY 10020

First Gallery Books hardcover edition March 2025

GALLERY BOOKS and colophon are registered trademarks of Simon & Schuster, LLC

For information about special discounts for bulk purchases, please contact Simon & Schuster Special Sales at 1-866-506-1949 or business@simonandschuster.com.

The Simon & Schuster Speakers Bureau can bring authors to your live event. For more information or to book an event, contact the Simon & Schuster Speakers Bureau at 1-866-248-3049 or visit our website at www.simonspeakers.com.

Interior design by Hope Herr-Cardillo

Manufactured in the United States of America

10 9 8 7 6 5 4 3 2 1

Library of Congress Cataloging-in-Publication Data has been applied for.

ISBN 978-1-6680-6197-8
ISBN 978-1-6680-6199-2 (ebook)

In loving memory of Martha Caldwell

PART I

CHAPTER 1

I'M TRYING TO THINK OF HOW to describe this room in a way that's not only accurate but also does it justice. I like to be deliberate with my words. I don't want to say *quaint* because that makes it sound like I'm talking about a cute little mom-and-pop sandwich shop in Portland, Maine. It's not cozy, it's not warm . . . if I'm being perfectly honest, it's not even nice.

There is a wooden coffee table that looks handmade, but the chairs are clearly from IKEA. There is a barren countertop with nothing but a French press and a stainless steel toaster. I guess they are going for a minimalist thing. The fridge is completely stocked with Dasani bottled water and one Red Bull, which I'm assuming is not mine for the taking. The decorations are subtle, but they scream southern charm, which makes me feel at home. There is one of those tacky tricolor braided rugs under the coffee table that looks like it's traveled to a few homes in its day. Then on the table is The Lantern.

You know the one I'm talking about. The varnish is completely gone from the wooden handle, there is a crack in one of the panes, and there is a hint of kerosene in the air. I don't know if this is done on purpose, if it's accidental, or if it's to send a message, but I definitely feel safer seeing it. I think that's the best word to describe this room . . . *safe*.

You know that feeling you get when you are waiting to see the dentist for a checkup? It's not like you're nervous because you're getting work done. You're nervous because you feel like you should be. This is where I am right now. I'm just plain nervous. I'm afraid I might say something stupid and embarrass myself. I'm afraid I might upset or offend her in some way, but then again she's clearly not fragile. It's kinda funny that a person can go through everything she has gone through and I think I have the power to ruin her day. Nevertheless, I want to be as respectful as possible while still allowing her to be a human and not an idol.

For me she is America's first Black superhero. If intuition, foresight, and navigation can be considered superpowers she is basically an Avenger. One of the big ones. She is Iron Woman. I can only imagine what it must be like to be her.

The social pressure, the responsibility, of being an icon. I know I shouldn't, but I walk over to the lantern and grab it. I bring it level with my eyes and imagine I am going through the woods of Dorchester County, Maryland.

Dogs are fresh on my heels and I keep fainting every couple of days. All the other runaways don't know if they should go on without me or if they should wait. One of them is very nervous and decides that he might run and go back out of fear, and the others tell him he better not even think about it or he'll have me to deal with. I am so worked up at this point I am fully screaming. "If you hear the dogs," I yell, "keep going! If you see the torches in the woods, keep going! If there's shouting after you, keep going! Don't ever stop! Keep going! If you want a taste of freedom . . . "

The door to the room swings open and I am snapped out of my little dream and she is standing right there. I am so embarrassed, but I'm also so excited. She is standing between two huge bodyguards. Actually, they are standing so far away I can't tell if they are huge or if she is tiny. She looks practically half their size.

"Please put that down," she says as I stand frozen.

"Ms. Tubman, I can explain," I say, gently placing the lantern on the table, only to realize I couldn't explain and should just try and salvage what's left of this introduction.

"I am so pleased to meet you. My name is Darnell. This

is truly a dream come true. I've been looking forward to this all week. You're my biggest inspiration. Whenever I feel like I can't go on I think—" She cuts me off.

"Look, baby." Harriet Tubman just called me "baby." "Thank you. Your words are kind, but we don't have all day." She is direct. This is what I expected from her, but it's still startling. She's now standing just about a yard from me. I could reach over and touch her if I wanted to. I want to. I really want to, but I don't. Mostly because she looks like she could and definitely would rip my hand clean off. But also, you just don't go around touching national treasures.

I never thought this day would come. When so many figures from the past started returning, I just kept hoping that Harriet would show. Not only did she show, but she reached out to me. I still have the invite she sent me, a lovely little handwritten note: *Nigga, get over here. —Harriet Tubman*. With the address of the studio. I think I'll have it framed.

It's been a very strange news cycle since The Return. Cleopatra is now an Instagram model, Rockefeller is having public battles of wealth display with Elon Musk and Jeff Bezos, and everyone is waiting on pins and needles to see if Jesus will return. I'm not betting on it.

Of all the people who have come back, I am the most excited about Harriet Tubman. She is beautiful, but it is an unconventional beauty. Her hair is like a dry wool helmet that's been parted down the middle. Even the skin on her scalp has scars and looks worn. Her skinny little hands are covered in veins and the skin looks like leather. She reaches out to shake my hand and it feels like holding one of those tiny New Testaments. Her clothes are all different shades of brown. Her dress looks like maybe it used to be black, but over time it's gotten dirty and weatherworn. The kind of distressing white kids used to pay way too much money for in the early 2000s at Aeropostale or Abercrombie. She does not look like she has had an easy life. But at the same time she truly looks like she is conquering it.

She wears pain, pride, and dignity on her face all at once. She has one of those faces that looks like she has always been old. Never seen a young or carefree day in her life. An "all's my life I've had to *fight*" face. She has a sort of permanent scowl. Now that I think about it, I don't think I've ever seen a picture or heard tell of her smiling, laughing, or even so much as letting out a slight chuckle. To say the very least, she is intimidating. A tiny little five-foot woman who is clearly in charge of this room.

"Hi . . . It's, uh, really good to meet you," I begin again, nervous to be reprimanded a second time by Harriet Tubman. "I don't usually fall over my words like this, but this is a dream come true. I didn't really expect to get a call from you of all people. I didn't even know if this was a prank or something. I'm glad I came down to see what this was all about."

I pause and wait for her to respond, but she doesn't say anything at all. She is very comfortable with uncomfortable situations. She never breaks eye contact with me. Not even for a second. I don't even think she has blinked since she entered the room. I know her eyes have to be dry. For a second, I consider offering her my Visine, but I'm already treading on thin ice.

She patiently stands there listening as I try and gather my thoughts for another minute or so, then she finally interrupts me and says, "Darnell." Hearing her say my name sends a jolt of adrenaline coursing through my spine. It's like I'm in high school and I've just been called to the principal's office.

"I wants to talk to the new generation. I wants to talk to Black folk today, and I think you might be just the person to help me reach them."

"Me?" I say, completely confused. "What could you want with me? I genuinely don't see how I could help you." This doesn't even make sense to me. Well, I certainly don't understand why she called me here, let alone how I can help Harriet Fucking Tubman. "But you're . . . you're Harriet Fucking Tubman!"

I really thought I said that in my head. But based on everyone's reaction, guess not.

"Please pardon my language."

"You think I haven't heard worse?" she snaps back. "I called you here because I need your voice and your ear." She grabs my hands and takes a very dramatic pause. "I've decided to make an album and I . . . "

"STOP!" I have to pause for a second. You know that feeling when you can't tell if you are in on the joke or if you are the joke? "Are you being serious? Like what kind of album?" It feels like I'm the first person outside of everyone in this room to hear this information. Harriet looks at the two huge bodyguards, who I am now realizing are the same height as me, and motions for them to wait outside. They leave the room in perfect synchronization, like members of some sort of elite military force.

"I wants to blend hip-hop and spirituals together. I'm tryna bridge the gap between you and yo ancestors. The songs we sang are your true history. They tell you everything about how smart, strong, creative, and resourceful you can be. And the music of today tell me everything about how far we come. What we done achieved. What we can own. I don't think you understand the power of owning something. Of actually having something you can call your own, and yo history." She pauses to look at me. "Yo history is yours, and can't nobody take that from you."

"But why me?"

"When tha Lawd tell you who to choose you don't ask no questions. I listened to the Lawd for over ninety years. Listenin' to tha Lawd helped me save over seven hundred of yo ancestors. Listenin' to tha Lawd helped me stay safe for thirteen trips back 'n' forth. Listenin' to tha Lawd has given me everythang I got. So when tha Lawd told me to send fa you . . . I didn't ask questions. And you shouldn't either."

I don't know what to say. I'm afraid to tell her I don't believe in God. If she was anyone else I'd look her in the eye and say, "Religion is the biggest scam on the face of the planet, followed closely by higher education in America." Then we'd engage in a thriving debate, though I'm afraid she'd just turn around and leave the room. I look up to her as if she is the matriarch of my family. She has the strength of an army and the warmth of a family, so I'm still afraid to disappoint her.

"Yas ma'am, I understand that," is all I can muster. This is silly. I feel like a child being preached to by one of the elders in my church, and I just nod in agreement while silently thinking I'm too smart for this. She reaches up and snaps her fingers right in front of my eyes.

"You listening to me?"

I realize that I am NOT listening at all.

"Yes ma'am!" I lie, and lie quickly.

"We gon' be spending a lot of time together. I'm gonna

need you on your A game. You better keep it together." As if on cue, the guards reenter the room. Every one of their moves looks like it's been choreographed. It's very impressive for two people this large to be so in sync.

"We gotta head to the stage. I wanna show you what I been working on. This where we gon' do the first show. We got a couple of spaces here in this building, and I hope we got everything you need to help us out. Now let's go." She doesn't check to see if I agree, or if I'm "in on the deal," she just starts moving. They don't even look back to make sure I'm following along. Of course I follow. I'm too curious to leave a party without hearing the next song, you think I'd pass up on an opportunity like this? I'm scrambling to keep up in the hallway.

She moves very fast for such a tiny person, and her dress touches the floor just perfectly so you can't see her feet. She does NOT have a delicate walk. She walks like Viola Davis in *How to Get Away with Murder* or Whoopi Goldberg in every film she's ever had to wear high heels in. Her stance is wide and her steps are deliberate. There is no question who is in charge of leading this caravan. She's walking about three feet ahead of the guards.

I finally catch up. "Are you going to tell me where we're going?"

Before she can answer, we're already there. She walks

me into a rehearsal room with a live band, backup singers, and a huge DJ booth in the shape of an H. I can't believe she is serious.

"This my band. They called the Freemans." I take a good look at her band and they are a motley crew. They look like they have returned as well. "They all made up of people I done helped and people that done helped me." She walks over to the only other woman in the room. "This Odessa. We met during the Combahee Ferry Raid."

Odessa looks like she couldn't be more than thirty years old. She doesn't look aged and worn down like Harriet. She looks to me like she has never done a hard day's work in her life. She is light-skinned with thick, wavy hair in a neat little bun. There is a beige ribbon holding the bun together with a thick decorative net over her hair to keep it in place. Clearly she is mixed race.

"Chile, even house slaves wanna run. You don't even wanna know what you gotta do to stay in the house when you a pretty girl like Odessa. She helped take part in her own liberation that night and ain't never looked back since. Plus, this child can sing."

Odessa looks at me sheepishly, then asks, "Is it true you wrote 'Bad Bitch Boot Camp'?"

"And produced . . . " I say, my confusion turning to horror as she begins rapping the Lil Genie song about "basic training these hoes" and how she's going to "ten hut a slut" in front of Harriet Tubman.

"All right, that's enough, Odessa," Harriet says. "I gave her some of your music to listen to and she hasn't stopped since."

I'm so embarrassed. That song is over twenty years old. From a different life. "I can explain . . . about that song," I begin to tell Harriet, apologetically.

"I liked it, but I prefer that song you did with Dr. Slim." I wince at the name, but a part of me is screaming. Harriet Tubman likes my music!

Harriet walks over to a big mandingo-looking mother-fucker. "This Buck. They call him Buck cause he strong. He plays the guitar." Now, Buck is scary. He's as wide as he is tall and has arms thick as his thighs. He is completely bald and his skin is so shiny that it's hard not to comment on. He is impressive. He looks like if Michael Clarke Duncan ate Michael Clarke Duncan. Despite his massive and intimidating frame he has the softest eyes I think I've ever seen on a person.

"He don't talk much, but this man smarter than most people I know. A lot of folks have ideas about you before they even get to know you? Um . . . what you say they call it, Buck?"

Buck lifts his head very slowly and rumbles: "Preconceived notions." His voice sends chills down my spine.

"Das right, 'preconceived notions.' I like the way colored folks talk today. Back in my day the only Negro talked like that was Frederick Douglass, and let me tell you right now. Most Negroes didn't like Frederick Douglass anyhow!"

This really takes me for a spell, because I didn't take Harriet Tubman to be the gossiping type! Now I want all the Frederick Douglass tea. "Ms. Tubman, why didn't Black folk like him?" I ask.

"Please don't 'Ms. Tubman' me. You really don't gotta be so fancy with me. You can call me Minty. That's what everybody else call me anyhow. I don't like all these formalities. It's too much." This is the first time I've been unafraid since we met. I feel like I can let my guard down a little. Up until now it's felt like an interview for a job that I KNEW I wasn't qualified for. Now I feel more at ease . . . and I wanna gossip.

"So Minty." I can't believe I just called her "Minty." "Why did people hate Frederick Douglass?" She turns her head with her lips pressed together, head slightly tilted, and one eyebrow raised.

"Now I didn't say 'hate.' You up here adding stuff. Everybody respected Frederick Douglass. Even racist white folks." She paused to find the most appropriate words. "They was jealous. He could read, he could write, was educated, light skin, that was enough. They thought he was uppity. When you told that you supposed to be low you sure don't wanna be down there by yourself." This seems to resonate with the other people in the room. Even I can relate to that.

"Now this good man right here is DJ Quakes," she says, taking me over to a tiny man behind a mixing board. "We call him that 'cause he a Quaker. And our DJ." It's kinda strange to see someone dressed like this in real life. The first thing you notice about him is that he is very short. When I say "very short" I don't mean "short for a man," I mean short for anyone. He is about four feet tall. His arms are the same length as his legs, and he is barrel chested. He is a little person. He also has a huge gray unkempt beard that connects seamlessly with his hair and eyebrows. He almost looks like a lion because it's all connected in one big mane. And his clothes look exactly how you think they look. A blackish-brown coat that goes down to his knees, with a dark-brown long shirt underneath, off-white socks that cover his calves, and a wide-brim hat that looks like it was once black that dips down at the center of his forehead. He is a sight to behold. He walks with a wooden cane that doesn't have a handle. It's basically a stick. And his voice is a little nasally. The kind of nasal voice that could easily be annoying if you didn't like the person, but lucky for me I really like him so far.

"A lot of folks don't know that Quakers helped a lot of us get to freedom, and they good, God-fearing people. Really believe in the Bible. I like that . . . "

As Harriet kinda trails off rambling about something or other, a skinny little man that is literally standing in her shadow clears his throat to bring her back to reality.

"Oh my goodness. Where are my manners? This my pride and joy. I love this man so much. He the one that helped me see we don't have to be property. This my baby brother, Moses. Our drummer." His eyes aren't exactly sad per se, but you wouldn't feel comfortable being less than kind to him. Everything he is wearing is some shade of brown. And his hat is . . . well, I don't want to say raggedy . . . but fuck it, his hat is tore up. There is an entire chunk of the brim missing in the back.

"I am so grateful for this one. Every time I look over at him I'm reminded that we gets to be free." She's clearly starting to get choked up, so she quickly moves on. He doesn't seem to mind the awkwardness. He kind of looks at the floor while she talks about him, occasionally gazing up to make eye contact. In spite of his tore-up brim, Moses somehow looks the fanciest out of everyone here.

"Well, anyway, this my band. We Harriet Tubman and the Freemans."

At this point I have a million questions.

Why a band? Why music? Why me? Why now? But instead I just say, "I'd love to hear what you've got."

So she directs me to a very uncomfortable plastic chair and makes her way to the stool in the middle of the room. She seems nervous to perform for me. It seems out of char- acter for her. There is a feeling in the air, and I can tell that I am the first person outside of everyone else in this room to hear whatever it is I'm about to hear. I also prepare myself in case it's horrible. What if Harriet Tubman and the Freemans play a song and it's truly no good? Then what am I going to do? Do I smile and say "good job," or does she genuinely want my input?

"I have to ask," I chime in before they get underway. "What do you want from me in this moment? I just want to be on the same page about why I'm here." There is a slight pause and everyone looks at each other as if they are just now deciding my purpose in this room. Tubman takes a few moments while pacing and really thinks to herself. Then she looks me straight in the eye and says, "For now . . . I just want you to listen."

"That all sounds great," I assure her. She walks over to the group and decides to lead them in prayer. I can't tell if I'm supposed to join, or just bow my head from a distance.

You know that awkward feeling you get when someone starts talking about Jesus, assuming you're a believer, without checking in with you first? That's how I feel. They all hold hands in a circle and Minty begins the prayer. I immediately realize that she is NOT a quiet prayer and I realize that I am most certainly supposed to have my head bowed because she starts with the words "Bow your head!" and it is not a request.

"Lord Father Jesus, we thank you for this opportunity to share our gifts. Lord Jesus, we thank you for another day alive, Lord Jesus, and we thank you for giving us this chance to be together, Lord Jesus. Lord Jesus, please pour your spirit over this experience tonight, Father. May these words pour over the spirit of this young man watching us tonight, Lord Jesus, and the tips of our tongues with every word we speak. Let us do your will tonight and not ours, Lord Jesus. Amen!"

I try to keep my head down a little bit longer so everyone sees that I did indeed bow my head during the prayer.

Harriet looks right at DJ Quakes and says, "All right y'all . . . Let's do it."

The music is a combination of hip-hop, rock and roll, and Negro spirituals. The music fills the massive rehearsal hall like the floodgates on a dam have been lifted. It starts with DJ Quakes hitting a button on his DJ board and everyone swaying in perfect harmony. A blast of rock guitar and 808 drums feels like it's going to blow my hair back. Tubman grabs the mic from the stand and starts:

WANTED A CHANCE TO WRITE SOME GOOD MUSIC

I MEAN SOME HOOD MUSIC

I'M TALKIING 'BOUT I WISH A MOTHERFUCKER
      WOULD MUSIC

LIBERATE MY PEOPLE THROUGH THE SWAMPS AND THE
      WOODS MUSIC

NEVER WOULD HAVE MADE IT IF I DIDN'T KNOW I
      COULD MUSIC

NO BOOK SMARTS SO THERE WAS VERY
      LITTLE EDUCATION

BUT I MADE IT WITH A LITTLE BIT OF DIVINATION

GOT A CALL TO LIBERATE A GENERATION

SO LET ME SLOW DOWN IF YOU DON'T SEE
      THE CORRELATION

She sings as if Dr. Dre and Ella Fitzgerald had a daughter. Angry, strong, and smooth all at once.

"Well . . . " I must have just been staring at her for a solid thirty seconds after she finished the song without saying anything. Which is a longer time for silence than you'd think, especially after a performance.

"You got something to say or you just gon' sit there like a bump on a log?" Harriet asks.

I immediately start clapping. More than anything I'm relieved because I was afraid that I might not like it. That would've made for a terrible day.

"Can't you say a word or two?" she adds.

"Sorry, I'm gathering my thoughts," I quickly reply. "I think this is amazing. I'm still not sure what you want from me, though. It already seems like you have a handle on things."

She looks at the Freemans, then back at me. "Baby, we stuck. I ain't never been too proud to ask for help and that's why you here tonight. You gon' help me write the rest of the album and the show telling my life story. Tha Lawd already told me you was the one. Once we write it we have to share it with the world. Release the album and go on a national tour."

I recoil at the thought. "ME! Why me? All I've ever written is a couple of club bops. And that was a lifetime ago. This feels like something different. It seems more serious."

She stomps over and grabs my hand. She is stronger than her tiny frame suggests. "I already done told you, when tha Lawd tells me I don't ask questions. I just get into action. Now what you gon' do?"

I just keep staring at them and then I say, "Can I step out back to clear my mind, please?"

She motions for me to go ahead. "You do what you gotta do. We'll be right here."

As I burst into the alley I'm trying to figure out how I even ended up in this situation. A few days ago, I was just sitting at home minding my own business, then all of a sudden I'm being propositioned to help bring Harriet Tubman's music and message to the masses.

As I frantically pace the alley, Moses comes out to see how I'm doing.

"Hey!" He has such a soft speaking voice. He seems like one of those people who have never raised their voice. "You mind if I hang out with you for a sec?"

As if I was gonna say anything but yes, he leans against the wall and pulls out a cigarette from a dingy flat tin case. It really matches his whole aesthetic. As he leans against the brick wall to light up he looks like a Norman Rockwell painting. Well, if Norman Rockwell had ever painted Black people.

"What's the matter?" he says as he lights his cigarette. He smokes like an old mechanic who's about to overcharge you on some automotive work you don't need, with the cigarette dangling on the edge of his lip. It is kind of hypnotic. Between his soft voice, sad eyes, muted clothing, and mesmerizing cigarette choreography I feel like I am being bewitched into a calm state.

"I don't know if you're the person I should even be talking to, but this is just all too much. This doesn't feel weird to you . . . AT ALL?! I don't know how to tell Harriet that I idolize her. I don't even know if I can stay professional throughout this whole project. I don't even make music anymore! I haven't written a song in almost ten years. I never even got around to writing my own story let alone someone else's. I feel like you all chose the wrong person, and there's a lot y'all don't know about me."

Moses slides his cigarette between his pointer and middle finger, snuffs it out on the wall behind him, and slides the remains into his pocket. He heads back into the building, and before the door closes behind him he stops it with his dirty, worn-down boot and tells me exactly what I need to hear.

"Man, ain't nobody judging you."

CHAPTER 2

"OKAY!" I SAY AS I WALK back into the room with a big burst of energy and a grin that's stretching clean across my face. I must look a mess. I know that my eyes are red from rubbing my face. I've unbuttoned the top button on my shirt. My palms are so sweaty.

"What you mean 'okay'?" Harriet stares at me with her thin eyebrows furrowed.

"I'll do it. I want to help," I say.

"Oh. Darnell, I wasn't asking. This ain't no negotiation. We on a mission from tha Lawd and I need you to start looking at it that way. Now . . . how we gon' get started?"

The band is looking directly at me, and I realize that I am now the captain of this ship. I look right back at Harriet.

"Tell me what you want your music to be about," I say,

and she retracts her head and makes that face Black people make when someone says something confusing.

"I want it to be about me!" she says. She doesn't just say it, she proclaims it. On the word *me* she stamps her tiny little foot down and lands in one of the poses she has in the very few photos that exist of her.

"Well, I understand that, but we aren't making an after-school special, are we? I assume you also want a point of view, a through line, chronology, etc." I can tell she hadn't thought that far in advance, and Odessa is making the "I told you so" face behind Tubman's back.

"Okay, let's start from the beginning. I think if you take a moment to just tell me about a few massive landmarks in your life I can work from there." Then I turn my attention to Harriet and the Freemans. "And I want to talk to all of you. Every single one of you is a part of Black history." This is definitely a warm moment that we are sharing together, when you can just feel the Blackness in the air. Then DJ Quakes walks into the room and pauses mid-doughnut bite. We all pivot toward him in unison.

"Umm . . . " he says, unsure exactly of what he's walked into. "I'm gonna go grab some coffee. Anyone want anything?" Everyone just stares at him as he backs out of the room silently.

We break up into pairs and I begin chatting with them

all one by one, starting with Odessa. I don't know what to ask without sounding offensive so I just rip the Band-Aid off and dive right in.

"Ms. Tubman said that you were a house slave?"

She nods as if that was a compliment. "I was. I worked on William Cruger Heyward's plantation on the Combahee River in South Carolina."

She smiles a lot, and is talkative and affectionate with her touch. I'd be interested in seeing her Myers-Briggs results. There seems to be a large amount of conditioning that makes her such a people pleaser. It doesn't come off as people-pleasing as much as it comes off as a survival technique.

"I sure hate that he died before Emancipation. Wish I could've seen his face when they told him he had to let go of his most 'prized possessions,' " Odessa says, her sweetness turning slightly sour. "And that's the problem. His most prized possession was the antithesis of mine. Mine was freedom. I hate to even talk about being a house slave too much, it just riles up controversy and arguing among Black folks. I think field slaves think we had it easy in the house, and that about enough to drive a person crazy." She takes the decorative net off her neat little bun and pulls the ribbon to let her hair fall, just to put it all back up again. It's like she's preparing to launch into an argument that she's had a million times before.

"Can you tell me some of the main differences between

being a house slave and a field slave?" I ask her. I feel really weird using the word *slave* around them. It feels like an insult.

She leans all the way forward in her chair, talking almost exclusively with her hands. "First of all, if you work in the fields you work sunup till sundown and—"

I jump right in, "That's terrible."

She shrugs as if to agree. "Yeah, it is, but when you in the house you work from the time you wake up till you go to sleep. There ain't no time off. Do you hear what I'm telling you? People think 'cause we indoors we living like white folks or something. No! We break our backs cleaning up after not just children but grown-ass adults too. All the food, every dish, entertainment, baths, mopping, sweeping, laundry, plus trying to stay the hell away from master and his son at all cost."

I can tell she is starting to get irritated, so I decide to shift the conversation. "And they never cooked for themselves?"

She just straight-up laughs at my question. "Harriet, you heard what this boy said?" she yells across the room.

"What he say?" she yells back.

She repeats my question and everyone in the room doubles over in laughter.

"Chile. Mrs. Heyward ain't know how to cook. She didn't even know how to use the stove. If it was up to her to feed them children they'd have been skinnier than a fiddle. Let me tell you something. White folks not seasoning they food did not start at the turn of the century. I never understood how they could even make bad food. They had the best slices of everything. Rich white folks wasn't eating chicken. They was eating hog and cow meat. Then they would throw us the scraps. That's the real challenge, trying to feed your whole family on a tiny chicken, hog intestines, and brain. All that food that make your mouth water we didn't feel none too lucky to be eating at the time. Oxtail, hog maw, chitterlings, gizzards, pig feet, chicken necks. You over there smacking your lips and we was trying to figure out how to make it all make sense." The way she describes it sounds like a fucked-up episode of *Iron Chef*.

"Then they turn around one hundred years later and tell you that they like what you made with the scraps. Chile, white folks don't know what they want." She sucks her teeth. Now all I can think about is Paula Deen on TV acting like she came up with southern cooking. Just adding a stick of butter to every recipe we had.

Odesssa really has the others going. I'm mostly hungry at this point, so I suggest we grab a bite, just the two of us. All this talk of pig intestines got me hungry for some traditional southern cooking, and since we're in Harlem, the northern capital of Soul Food, USA, I take her to the famous Sylvia's. It's only three blocks away, but Odessa stays close enough for me to smell the coconut oil in her hair all the way there, her eyes darting around this magical new world I'd only thought of as Harlem. But I forget Odessa and the others only just returned, all of this twenty-first-century life must be overwhelming.

That, and walking down any street in New York is enough to send anyone not used to it into a state of absolute panic. I offer Odessa my hand and she takes it almost gratefully.

"Don't you ever get lost round here? All these people and buildings and . . . is that dog feces?" I look down just in time to avoid what may or may not be dog shit.

"Let's hope so," I say as we wait for the light to cross one of those wide streets with too many lanes. "I used to, when I first moved here, but that was over twenty years ago. But sometimes, if I'm not looking, I can turn down a strange corner and end up in a place I've never seen." All the zooming cars and loud honking and yelled epithets and truly evil bike riders has her a little jumpy.

"Do you get scared?"

"No." She feels like a little sister, even if she's technically one hundred fifty years, and some change, older than me. "I kinda like getting lost. It helps me . . . forget."

"Forget what?" I look down at Odessa and her eyes are trained on me. I want to tell her everything but instead I say nothing and usher her across the street, which immediately consumes all of her attention. She runs across the street like she's back on the Underground Railroad.

"Woo, Lawd, I didn't think we'd make it!" She's trembling but, I can tell, excited. "This place sure is something!" Is it? There's an unhoused gentleman peeing on the new Chanel store that opened last month and now he's getting yelled at by a Chanel employee . . . oh wait, I think that's his boyfriend. This place is something.

At Sylvia's, there is a line, of course, snaking around the block but Odessa, not knowing any better—or just not caring—walks to the front of it. I bow my head, expecting shouts to take our Black asses to the back of the line, but to my surprise, everyone just lets us cut them. They recognize Odessa as one of "the Returned" and treat her like some sort of celebrity, some even snapping photos of her with their phones.

Odessa stands in the middle of the restaurant, deeply inhaling the familiar smells of oxtails and chitterlings. I tell her to get whatever she wants and I immediately regret that decision. She's tiny but she can really pack it away. She's then shocked when all that food is ready in a few minutes. "Back in the day, I woulda been cooking all day!" she marvels.

The way Odessa's eyes light up when she bites into that deep fried chicken, you'd think it was the greatest thing she ever tasted. I try to ease back into conversation, but the way she looks at me when I try to talk to her, I decide it's best to wait. After she scarfs down one of everything from the menu, by her lonesome, she looks at me with a strange look.

"You must think I'm crazy." I don't. If I suddenly showed up one hundred fifty years in the future, I wouldn't know what's up from down. I think she's doing remarkably well. Considering. "What do you do with all of this?"

"All of what?"

She looks at me with that strange look again. "All of this freedom?"

Her question nearly knocks the air out of my lungs. If only because I don't have an answer for her. Instead of answering her question, I ask one of my own. "When did you realize that you *could* be free?"

She pauses a moment to think about the answer. "If I'm being honest, I don't think I believed I'd be free from my bondage till I set foot in Philly. Even then, I didn't believe it till I finally heard about the signing of the Emancipation Proclamation. Being enslaved is not the kind of experience you can easily shake. At least it wasn't for me. It's not like I was caught and then got enslaved. My momma was a slave, and her momma, and her momma, too, far as I know. Wasn't no free folk in my family line that I ever remembered. It's locked in your bones and blood. It's in your DNA. It done made its way all the way down to you. When Harriet and the 54th Massachusetts Infantry Regiment came onto the plantation that day it was glorious. I've never seen anything that beautiful in my life. I was paralyzed with fear, joy, excitement, pain, just about every feeling a person can have all at once. There is just madness going on around me. And I heard muskets firing and people screaming. I overheard somebody say, 'Harriet's here!' Every slave worth a nickel knew about Harriet. This the most famous Black person alive next to Frederick Douglass—not that his uppity ass would ever come see *us*."

· · ·

I thought we should head back to the studio, but Odessa wanted to walk around some more. She loved seeing what the new world has to offer. I felt envy that a restaurant in Harlem could look anything but ordinary.

"There were so many rumors flying around about Harriet," she continued, between licks of her new obsession, frozen yogurt. "Most people thought she was a man. Some people thought John Brown had somehow faked his death and was operating in Black face. Some people even thought she was a spirit, 'cause they couldn't figure how she hadn't been caught yet. When I heard Harriet was there I ran toward the trouble like a damn fool. Everybody was running the opposite direction I was running, but I had to see what

Harriet looked like! Was she tall and strong? Was she a little man? Was she a ghost? I felt like I couldn't do nothing else until I was looking her in the eye." Her face is bright and alive as she speaks.

"Folks was trying to pull me back in the other direction, but I kept moving into the crowd. After pushing my way through the madness I finally saw her. She was standing there holding a rifle with a bayonet on the end that was taller than she was. I don't know how I knew that was her, but I just knew. I ain't never seen a woman with that much power, let alone a Black woman. I asked her, 'You Harriet?' and she just looked at me and said, 'You free.' "

Odessa's eyes are so wide and watery while she's telling this story. I can tell she is back on the plantation. She is not with me on this street. Her voice has calmed down almost to a whisper. She is no longer waving her hands frantically like she was when talking about the food. I can't tell if she is going to smile or cry. Maybe both. We sit on a park bench so Odessa can gather her emotions—though if I'm being honest, I need it as much as she does.

"It felt so quick, even though it took me my whole life to get there. With two words I was free. My eyes swelled up and it felt like I saw the face of God." Again I reach for Odessa's hand. She feels like home.

"Now I'm running through the chaos of the plantation

that used to be home with my eyes all watery and I can barely see. It felt like a metaphor for what was to come. How you supposed to know how to go about the world when you ain't never been in it? That's what they don't talk about. How I'm supposed to know about freedom when I was born a slave, and my momma was too? I felt like I been navigating the world with my vision obscured. Trying to keep up with white people with a four-hundred-year head start, plus when they cross the finish line they just keep dragging it with them. They call you lazy even though you work more than you sleep, they call you stupid even though you engineered food from garbage, and they call you dangerous without acknowledging their hand in the matter."

She pauses for a while and we just sit in silence, her tiny hand in mine. It doesn't feel awkward, it feels appropriate. I give her a moment to catch her breath and so I can catch mine. I've never thought about a runaway after they've run.

When we get back to the studio, I feel like Odessa and I have entered some secret pact together. So when Moses walks over and asks what we were talking about, I'm hesitant to tell him, but Odessa blurts out that she was just telling me about Emancipation. "Half the folks didn't even realize they was already supposed to be free by then. Hell, it ain't like slave masters would come by and give us the good news," he says, half chuckling to himself.

"That's for damn sure," Harriet adds.

This is really making me think. It really struck me that Odessa never thought she could be free. It was a goal that seemed so unattainable that she couldn't even fathom it until it was staring her right in the face.

"When did you start dreaming of freedom, Harriet?" I ask her. She looks at me like she's been waiting for me to ask this question for a hot minute now.

"I didn't always think I deserved to be free. Like everybody else in this room I was born in bondage, and I sure didn't like it, but it felt normal to me." I want to add that I had, in fact, not been born in bondage, and I didn't think Quakes had been either, but that seems beside the point, as well as an unnecessary and kinda cruel brag.

"And that was the main goal of the slavers, to make you feel like this is normal and to make you feel scared. This why they worked so hard to keep us ignorant. You know we wasn't allowed to read at all. Occasionally they would let one Black read and the only thing he could read was the Bible. They used him to preach us into subjugation. But you can't keep God people down for too long. Just like God brought the Jews through the desert, I knew he was gon' bring us through this. Let me tell you a story."

I'm very excited because I can tell Harriet is about to tell me one of her parables. I quickly run to get my notepad in case inspiration hits. I keep getting lost in these stories and forget I have a job to do. An important job.

"Moses, come over here!" she yells across the room. Moses walks over almost like he is embarrassed or shy. Harriet is holding him in a side hug, her hip significantly lower than his. She is talking to me, but she is maintaining very strong eye contact with him as he finds comfort in her loving grip.

"You see this man right here? He helped me learn my most valuable lesson in life when he was just a baby. Now, I'm one of nine. That's how they did us back then. You had to keep a slave fertile and making babies. Selling us like livestock. Chile, they didn't even see us as people, and if they showed even the slightest shred of mercy to us, they walked around acting like they was the Good Samaritan from Luke 10:25."

I'm not familiar. Maybe at one point I was, when I still considered myself a believer, but that was a lifetime ago and I've since rented that part of my brain out to *Love & Hip Hop: Atlanta* quotes.

"I always loved children even though I never had one myself," Harriet continues. "I mean, I have a daughter, but I adopted. I might as well have had children. Practically raised Moses like he was my own." Moses flashes me an uncomfortable glance and our eyes lock for what feels like too long. "I knew he was special 'cause the way my momma looked at him when he was born. Now I done watched them snatch up many of my brothers and sisters right from my momma's arms and sell them down the river, but when Moses was born, I reckon she couldn't take it no more. I think she knew she was getting too old to have more kids. That's a sad moment for a woman in chains."

"Why is it sad?" I ask. "Wouldn't they be happy to finally stop birthin' babies?"

"Happy? Oh naw. You think this might be your last chance to give life, and you already know the kind of life they gon' lead. Plus, once you done having children your fate gets even worse. Your workload gets heavier, they feed you less, because you are worth less to them."

I forget that they were merely property, investments, nothing more than cattle to their enslavers. Their lives had a dollar amount. Down to the penny.

"Right when Moses was born some man from Georgia came around talking about how he wanted to buy my brother. And you don't want to go down the river. Going deeper into the South is like going deeper into the pits of hell. Each county you pass is basically another level in Dante's *Inferno*."

Since we're all sitting around here in the studio, I get an idea. "Ms. Tubman, Harriet, Minty, sorry to interrupt you, but—"

"You ain't interrupting, speak your mind, baby."

"While you talk, can we get some accompaniment?" She looks at me confused, but before I can explain, Buck picks up his guitar and starts playing this beautiful lick. He looks to Harriet, gives her a nod, and she picks up where she left off.

"The man from Georgia had his eye on Moses, and we had our eyes on him. We all took turns hiding Moses around the plantation, in the woods, with other families. Whenever master or any suspicious-looking white man came around, we made sure Moses was not in sight. Well one day they must've caught us off guard because the man from Georgia was just standing in our doorway blocking out most of the light. He was a big ole man."

As Buck plays and Harriet tells her tale, the other Freemans gradually join in. First Odessa hums a delicate melody just under Harriet's words.

"My momma had run outta options. Either she was gon' let this man take her child or she was gon' do something about it. As he moved closer to Moses, my momma picked up a big stick we kept in the home for protection and raised it over her head."

The music stops and all the runaways make a grimace. "Why'd y'all stop? That was going so good!" They all just look at me blankly.

"I don't think you understand," Harriet says. "You can't stand up to no white man with words, let alone a weapon. I thought my momma was about to die right then and there, but then I saw something I ain't never seen before. He stopped dead in his tracks." I imagine it was like when Celie put a curse on Mister in *The Color Purple*. "She said 'You are after my son, but the first man comes into my house, I will split his head open.'"

It seems like Buck had not heard this story before because he is sitting on the edge of his seat with his mouth agape.

"What he do?" he asks.

She turns to him with her eyes as wide as they can go and she says, "He left . . . You hear me? He turned around and left. God must have been looking over us on that day, 'cause Lord knows I've seen people get lynched for less than that. I had never seen a white man afraid of a woman, let alone a Black woman. In that moment I realized I was powerful, too. On that day my momma decided she was gon' do whatever it took to make sure her baby had the best life she could provide. That was the day I decided I wasn't 'bout to be no slave for the rest of my life. I didn't have a plan or nothing, but I knew that freedom was the only option for me."

I think I'm starting to see it now. Now I understand why this seems like such a big moment. To realize that there is more than just one existence, that there's more to life than being someone else's property. To realize that you are your own person, capable of your own actions, able to create your own dreams, and with them, your own world. These are the little things we don't consider if we were never enslaved, things you don't even bother to think about when you are born free. I'm now on the edge of my seat, too. "So what did y'all do after he left?" I ask.

"My momma turned to me and said, 'Now you see,' and I don't think I'll ever forget that." She pauses for a minute to really let the words sink in again after all these years.

"What did she mean by that?"

"I ain't too sure, if I'm being honest. We never talked about it again. Some things you just don't go on and on about when you trying to stay alive. Maybe she meant, 'Now you see you got power, too' or maybe she meant, 'Now you see not to fuck with me.' Hell I know. I just took it as 'Now you see we are people too.' "

I run over to my backpack and open my laptop. I turn to DJ Quakes. "Could you give me a staccato violin beat?" Harriet has such a rhythmic pattern to her speech that I could hear the beginnings of a song in her story. "And add some bass under it." Everyone starts to look at me as my head bops up and down to Quakes's beat and I scribble furiously on the notepad. It always makes me uneasy when people watch me work so I turn my back to them like a petulant child and continue jotting down words as Quakes plays the instrumental track in the background.

I start to say the words I've written, sync them to Quakes's track:

AS SHE STANDS IN THE DOORWAY HUFFIN' AND
    SWEATIN'
REALIZING SHE'S FIERCE BECAUSE HER BABY HAD BEEN
    THREATENED
I SEE A WOMAN AT HER WITS' END

It starts to come together. The flow and rhythm of the words. The music matching and pushing me.

I NEED AMAZING GRACE. HOW SWEET THE SOUND?
DON'T WANNA TURN THIS PLACE INTO MY BURIAL
    GROUND
I ONCE WAS LOST, BUT NOW I'M FOUND
GOTTA PUT A PLAN IN ACTION, I'M NOT FUCKING
    AROUND
YOU SEE I ONCE WAS BLIND, NOW I SEE

I think this might work.

CHAPTER 3

SINCE MY CAREER BLEW UP IN my face years ago, I've had a sinking feeling of dread in my stomach. A medium-size stone in my gut, and I've gotten so used to that weight, that dread, that I didn't even realize its burden until it was lifted slightly.

I left the studio feeling more alive than I have in years. I have . . . a purpose. I take the subway to my place. My home is a shitty little studio in Morningside Heights, the Siberia of Manhattan. It's all I can afford these days, but it's mine. And that's something.

I just keep thinking about Harriet and Odessa and the other Freemans, about what they went through and about . . . how much I owe them. Just as a Black person. I'll never be able to pay them back for the sacrifices they made, but this project could be a start. Harriet believes in it, believes in me, for some reason. I jot down some more ideas for a couple hours before falling asleep to the always soothing sound of women fighting about nothing in particular on reality TV. Harriet Tubman believes in me. That makes one of us.

I arrive bright and early the next morning. I have way more energy than anyone should have at 9 a.m. without coffee. I'm still riding the high of writing my first song for Harriet Tubman and she seemed to like it. Well, as much as I could tell. After listening to "Now I See," she just looked at me, nodded, and went off somewhere to, I dunno, do Harriet Tubman things. What does she do with her free time?

"Good morning, everyone!" I say, breezing into the studio. "I've been thinking all night about where I want to start today. Odessa, you said something yesterday that has been stuck in my brain all night . . . " I take my backpack off, pull out my laptop, and remove my sunglasses only to realize that the only people here are me and DJ Quakes.

"Good morning. I am just finishing up my coffee," Quakes chirps. He also seems to be in a very good mood.

"Where is everyone?" I ask. It seems odd that no one else is here.

"It is Sunday . . . " He pauses. He expects me to understand what that means. He can clearly see my confusion because we are just staring at each other.

"Okay! What is this, a Chick-fil-A?" I say sarcastically. He does not seem to get my humor. That makes sense. I guess he doesn't know what a Chick-fil-A is.

"Church. . . . Everyone is at church." He finishes his coffee in one swig.

"Ohh." It didn't even occur to me that anyone would be in church right now. I haven't been to church in over a decade. I've actually been afraid that Harriet and her crew would think I was something of a heathen. I know she is devoutly religious, and let's just say that I'm afraid she wouldn't agree with my lifestyle, so I've kept certain aspects of my personality to myself. And if I'm being honest, that doesn't seem fair. She has been so forthcoming with me. Telling me extremely personal things. I really admire her conviction. I am so used to code-switching that sometimes I don't even know who I am anymore. Her ability to be herself through it all is next level. I get uncomfortable around religious people though. Full disclosure: Religious people annoy the shit out of me. Even when they aren't preaching it feels so preachy.

It all seems a little too aggressive for me at times. I grew up in the South and I was raised Southern Baptist, but not in a "hellfire and brimstone" way. In more of a "we condemn the sins of others without actually working on ourselves" way. You know the people.

All is forgiven at the end of the day if you just ask for forgiveness. So with that in mind, you can lie, fornicate, cheat, drink, and steal all you want because you get a blank slate at the end of the day with your whiskey sour nightcap. All you need is just a sprinkle of forgiveness from the divine mixed in with your bitters. I've never been able to reconcile what it means to be Black, queer, and American all at once.

If you aren't rejected for one thing, it's another. My family and I don't really talk much about my personal life, so I certainly don't find it easy to talk to others about it, unless I am onstage in front of a great big audience or paying someone $120 an hour. So, like I always do when I am uncomfortable with my feelings, I ask Quakes about himself.

"Why aren't you at church?" I ask. "Aren't you super religious?" All I knew was that he was a Quaker, not that I really know what that means.

"I am a Quaker. We do not do church services that you might be used to," he says calmly.

"You have to forgive me. I don't know much about your religion. I don't think I've ever even met a Quaker in real life." What I don't tell him is that all I know about Quakers is from a box of oatmeal.

"Well, let me tell you a little bit about myself." He pulls up a chair and starts in on his oatmeal muffin, and no the irony is not lost on me. "My actual name is Benjamin Lay, but everyone calls me Little Benjamin, because, as you can see, I'm smaller than most." For some reason it hadn't occurred to me that his name isn't actually DJ Quakes. "I am from Britain originally but I came to America in the early 1730s." He takes a comically large bite of his muffin and this time he starts talking while he is chewing with crumbs falling all over his beard, but in a charming way. "You should be a Friend. Come to a meeting someday. You might find that you like it."

I recoil at the thought of sitting in on a religious ceremony and enjoying myself. I must have a snarl or something on my face because he says, "Don't knock it until you have tried it."

I immediately get defensive. Of course I have tried church. This isn't my first time thinking about Christianity. He can tell that I am in my feelings. He continues to eat his muffin. His clothes are a mess at this point. The muffin looks very large in his tiny hands.

"I have invited many people to meetings and they tend to feel a little differently when they leave," he says.

I don't think I will take him up on his offer, but I don't want to offend him. I just nod and smile. I've learned to do this throughout my life to keep the peace. My level of people-pleasing is through the roof. I've always been more interested in keeping the peace than getting the win.

I have to admit, he does make the idea of religion seem more attractive. Whatever he's got going on, he just seems so accepting. I'm almost compelled to tell him about myself. He gives his beard a shake and as the crumbs cascade down his homely clothes and onto the floor I suddenly feel very content with being vulnerable.

"I . . . I've never felt very accepted by the church," I start, hesitant but almost excited to share something of myself. It's still a new feeling. "So, I've just kind of written it off over the years. For good."

Quakes gets up, walks over to me, puts his miniature hand on my shoulder, and stares me deeply in the eyes. "I am so sorry to hear that. Religion should be a force for bringing people together, not tearing them apart."

I stare back until it becomes uncomfortable, which is only a couple seconds, then avert my gaze, suddenly embarrassed at both my admission and how much better I feel having said it. If no one else is here I'm not sure why I should be, but I already made the trip down here.

"Do you want to work on some tracks?" I ask Quakes.

"Actually," he says as he jumps up suddenly, "I am glad you are here!"

Confused, I respond, "I'm glad I'm here too?"

"No, no, I am glad you are right here, right now. I had a request to ask of you. I have been *deejaying* now for, oh, two weeks, and I admit, I find it wonderful."

Two weeks? This eighteenth-century dwarven Quaker

spins better than most professional deejays. Of course, most professional deejays are also models, influencers, and/or investment bankers on the side.

"I wish to take advantage of your superior ear. I have developed an affinity for vinyl records and wanted to know if you could recommend some interesting and worthwhile finds?"

I immediately get a raging nerd-boner. Quakes wants to talk records? I know exactly the place. After Quakes finishes removing traces of muffin from his beard—I swear more got in there than in his mouth—I take him to my favorite record store, Luke's on 135th. They have the best selection in the city and they're kept open by the grace of someone's god and a rent-controlled storefront.

Unlike Odessa, Quakes seems completely unfazed by the modern world. Unfazed and unimpressed. He just charges forward, oblivious or indifferent to the stares that must be part and parcel of being a four-foot Quaker. But when we enter Luke's, he is astounded for the first time. Before I can tell him where anything is, Quakes is already rifling through crates. I like him.

Hours go by and I realize maybe the rest of the crew might be getting back from church soon, unless it's one of those twelve-hour services Black folks just seem to love. If it is, this day is shot. I dig Quakes out of some seventies funk

LPs and suggest we head back. We're both loaded down with records as we make our way into the studio. Still empty.

Quakes and I eagerly put on our latest finds and wait for everyone to get back. Quakes takes a small packet out of his jacket pocket and begins rolling what I assume is a cigarette. When he lights it, however, I remember that people have been getting stoned for centuries.

"Shouldn't we smoke this outside?"

"No one minds. Trust me," he says with a wink.

The studio is thick with smoke as LaBelle's 1974 opus *Nightbirds* (my choice) plays in the background. Quakes is such an interesting character, but something about him keeps nagging at me.

"Quakes," I say. "Why do you care so much about Black lives?"

He opens his eyes, sits up from his position on the floor, and looks at me with so much sincerity that tears start to well up in his eyes. He says, "I believe there is a light inside all living things. There is a little bit of God in all of us, therefore we are all worthy of respect." I guess he said the right thing at the right time, because I start tearing up too. Maybe somewhere down the line I forgot that I deserve respect too.

There's something about being told you're worthy from another person that feels better than when you tell yourself in the mirror. I don't want him to see my crying, so I turn around quickly and head to the watercooler, trying to change the subject without him hearing the quiver in my voice.

"So tell me about your church service," I say while wiping tears from my eyes. I make it look like I'm just rubbing my eyes, but I don't honestly think he's falling for it. I'm grateful that he's at least playing along.

"It is not a church; it is a meetinghouse. That is a very important distinction," Quakes tells me. "In churches you all sit facing the man in the robe who seems to feel that he is anointed by God to give advice to his subjects. Back in my day, women were not even allowed to talk in church at all. If you had a question about the Lord you had better save that thought in your pretty little head and remember to ask your husband when you got home. That does not sound like a direct path to God. You mean to tell me that the only way to God is through Jesus, and the only way through Jesus is through your husband, who has to first go through the pastor? That is either a long route to talk to your creator or somebody made up a bunch of rules to keep certain people in power, and to keep others submissive." He says all of this with a lot of pride, but it also seems like he has an axe to grind with other sects of Christianity.

"So what's the difference between a church and a meetinghouse?"

"Well, for starters, we all face each other," he says quickly.

This completely throws me off. That sounds more like an AA meeting than a religious service.

"And the pastor just spins in a circle to face everyone?"

"There is no pastor, no clergy, no deacon, no pope, no preachers, no teachers, no imams, no rabbi. We just have each other. We all minister to one another."

At this moment I am starting to realize that Quakers might be the original hippies.

"So you all just sit in a room and talk to each other?" The simplicity of it all seems really complex to me for some reason.

"We do not just sit around talking to each other. No. One at a time when the spirit moves you. When you feel that light inside of you stir, you stand up and you can address the room. Sometimes when the light stirs up in Friends their whole essence shakes and stirs. Your whole body begins shaking and quaking, and that's how we got the name Quakers. We are formally called the Religious Society of Friends. I guess God has gotten a little less dramatic over the years. Nowadays you just kind of stand up and start talking."

It sounds a little odd, but I can appreciate it.

"Well that's different from what I know. For sure," I tell him.

"As you can see I have always been at least a little different."

"It couldn't have been easy," I say, almost instinctively.

"When I first came to America I was politely asked not to return to a few meetinghouses because of my radical views."

I side-eye this strange little white man and ask, "What radical views?" I'm afraid I'm going to have to ask him where he was on January sixth.

"I was really shocked at America's views on slavery. Don't get me wrong, I have my gripes with the way England has treated people as well. That is part of why I decided to come here in the first place. When the spirit would move me, I would stand up and make my feelings known and I guess people didn't like that. That is how I ended up living in a cave right outside Philly."

"I'm sorry, what?"

"Yes, people always seem taken aback by the cave. After my beloved wife, Sarah, died, I sought to live a life that caused no harm to anyone or any thing. Besides, I got rejected by enough friends that I decided it would be easier to remove myself."

"I'm sorry about your wife."

"Thank you, Darnell. I truly believe there is a little bit of God in every living creature, even down to the lowly chicken. Which is why I'm a vegetarian."

This confirms my thoughts about them being hippies.

"I made my own clothes, grew my own food, even fixed up my own home. I never wanted anything to do with the infernal institution of slavery or the suffering of any of God's beautiful creatures." His voice is starting to get a little agitated, as if this is bringing up some bad memories for him. He grabs his cane and starts pacing back and forth on the hardwood floor. He has a very significant hobble. He really sways from side to side when he walks. The more upset he gets the more severe the sway becomes. Not just his sway but his breathing is getting pretty heavy too.

"Here, have a seat," I offer as I pull up a chair. I don't want him to get too upset. He's not really a spring chicken.

"Do not worry about me. I am as healthy as a Shetland. I just believe what I believe with vigor!" He rejects the chair and instead starts walking around it. "There were not a lot of people protesting slavery when I first arrived here. It was certainly not a popular opinion and won me very few friends, but luckily other Friends got on board. There were many anti-slavers living here in the colonies. You have runaways like Harriet and the others, free Negroes that opposed the institution, Quakers like myself, and more radical people like Harriet's old friend John Brown. We each had different ways of combating this poison coursing through the veins of our nation, but we each had the same goal." He starts to calm down a little.

The door swings open and it's Buck. His silhouette is so big that it blocks out the entire doorframe. There is just a sliver of light shining behind him with a spark at the top of the door like a solar eclipse.

"Buck, what are you doing here?" I ask. Now that I know about how they treat Sunday, I wasn't sure anyone would come in.

"I'm just stopping by to grab my coat. Harriet don't like for us to work on Sundays, so I just take that time off to myself." I guess it's just me and Quakes then. I'm a bit relieved, actually. Buck glides over to his coat. He is surprisingly smooth for a man his size, making it to the coat in about four steps. I swear it would've taken me ten.

"I thought you'd be in church singing hallelujah and praising the Lord," I say to him.

"Nah. Not my thing." He waves his massive hand. He doesn't even bother to look up when he says it. Didn't seem like a very big deal to him at all. Now me, on the other hand, this really throws me for a spell. I guess without considering it I just assumed that all enslaved people were deeply Christian. It felt like the truth without ever having it verified.

"What do you mean when you say it's not your thing?"

Seems like he is trying to make a beeline for the door. I can't tell if he wants to have this conversation or not, but I know that I do. He begins to walk and I put myself between him and the door, but he doesn't slow down at all. So I just move out of the way out of fear of being knocked over. He makes it to the door, and he stands there eclipsing the light again. I don't know where he is walking to. I have the only car in the parking lot.

"Sorry, I don't mean to be all in your business. I just want to get to know each of you a little better." Buck turns to face us.

"You sure you wanna hear my thoughts on God?"

I wasn't prepared for a warning. I mean how bad could his thoughts be? I imagine if he's giving out warning shots like this he must have gotten into a few heated discussions over his views.

"I would love to hear what you think, and I've got nothing but time. My day just freed up," I say to him.

"Okay . . . but if you call yourself a Christian and you're easily offended, this is your warning." He puts his coat on and bunches up the sleeves. His whole posture changes. It finally looks like he isn't running out the door. For some reason I feel uncomfortable for Quakes. Weird, right? Instead of being engaged in this conversation that I am sure is going to be interesting to say the least, my gut instinct is to feel protective of this institution that I'm not even sure I believe in. I guess bad habits die hard. As I glance back at Quakes he seems pretty unfazed. Maybe he has heard it all before. He also seems so strongly convicted in his own beliefs that nothing can waver him. I feel like a swing state during an election year, like I'm going to walk out on one side or the other. I don't feel this way because they are trying to convince me of anything. So far Quakes hasn't really tried to convert me or anything. I guess I feel that way because I'm looking for answers and I don't truly know what I believe in. It's hard to feel secure when you are standing between two men with such strong opinions.

"I've been ostracized by a lot of the Negro community because of my views on religion. Therefore I tend to keep my thoughts and ideas to myself," Buck says to me.

"Did your parents not teach you about religion?" I ask. His face scrunches as if he wants to assure me that I have indeed asked a very stupid question.

"Man, every slave in America done heard about Jesus. Whether we wanted to or not, and that's the truth. It just never made sense to me. My first memories are from church. If you could even call a run-down hut with a dirt floor a church. They made sure we went to church every Sunday, and they would read scripture to us while we was working out in the field."

It seems like all three of us have a grudge against the church, one way or another. Buck has said maybe three words to me up to this point, and now I don't think I could stop him from talking if I tried. Not that I would, as he's still like three times my size.

"Every slave knows Ephesians 6:5: 'Servants, be obedient to them that are your masters according to the flesh, with fear and trembling, in singleness of your heart, as unto Christ.' They would chant this over and over while lashing the whip in the air. As a field nigger you would hear this Bible verse every single day. You knew it better than you knew the names of the people you was laboring next to. That's the most disgusting part. The only verses I ever heard from the Bible were all text telling me to love my fellow man and worship my master. It all felt like a plot to keep me docile."

I'm kind of surprised to hear Buck talk like this. To hear any Black person born two hundred years ago talk like this. I guess I thought all slaves were obedient servants of the Lord. Slaves to white men and to their white god. Buck is definitely not that.

"At some point I understood that my servitude was my downfall and their greatest asset. I know it seems obvious from the outside, but when you in it . . . when it's all you know . . . it feels more than normal." I can hear his sadness beneath the bravado.

"See, my grandmother was Ashanti," Buck says after a short pause. "She was captured in Africa and brought to America. Not a lot of slaves had such a direct link to their heritage. It was never lost on me that all our customs and traditions were stripped from us. And when I say stripped I don't mean forgotten over time, I mean ripped from our hands and pried from our brains. They would literally tear your clothes off your body. When they would get you ready for the auction block they would give you the roughest shower of your life, then cover you in oil so you looked shiny and new."

I quiver at the thought. It's a shudder of unspeakable anger and sadness that anyone would have to go through that, let alone someone standing right in front of me.

"They would take your clothes and burn them or just throw them on the ground. I can't even imagine what it must have been like to come across the clothes of someone you loved just lying on the floor in a heap like they had been snatched away in the Rapture. Christianity always felt more like a punishment than a religion. It's a religion that has been forced on us and used as a tool to keep us poor and subservient for hundreds of years. So I'm sure that y'all can understand if I don't subscribe."

We all kind of just look at one another. Seems like Buck has been wanting to get this off his chest for a long time. Even though I don't disagree I feel compelled to defend Christianity.

"Maybe it's all part of God's plan." I don't think I realized what I was saying until the words had escaped me.

"Ugh," he grunts, and zips up his coat. I guess this conversation is over. Quakes and I awkwardly gather our things in silence.

Right when Buck gets to the doorway he turns around and calmly says, "If this is the plan, then God hates Black people."

He walks out of the room and lets the door close softly behind him.

CHAPTER 4

I HAD A LOT OF TIME to think about what Buck said. I think I've always felt the same way, but was never brave enough to say it out loud. Buck is truly free.

There is an old Nina Simone quote that goes, "I'll tell you what freedom is to me: no fear. I mean really, no fear!" Buck seems to have lost his feeling of fear. I really admire that. He doesn't seem to bother himself with what others will think of his opinions. I've found myself in so many scenarios where I felt the same way he does, but I just held my tongue. I was afraid to speak my true feelings out of fear that it would rock the boat or upset someone. And I lost a lot because of my fear.

Something about the way Buck let that door close behind him without even looking back stayed with me. He didn't check to make sure we were okay or anything. He just said what he said and let us sit with it.

As I walk in on Monday morning, I share a glance with Buck and Quakes. It feels like we had a strange trip to Vegas where everyone did something they were ashamed of, yet it bonded us. I enjoy the feeling. I don't feel so separated from everyone today. I'm beginning to feel less like an employee and more like a member of the group. I'm starting to feel like a runaway myself, but I don't know what I'm running from.

We're back in the reception area where I first met Harriet. Everyone is milling around making small talk and even chatting it up with me asking about my weekend. I didn't tell the others about coming in on Sunday. That felt private for some reason. The Red Bull must be here just for me because no one else has touched it.

Harriet is drinking black coffee out of a tin cup without a handle. This coffee is steaming and she's sipping it like it's an ice-cold glass of lemonade with condensation on the side. I'm deep in a serious conversation with Moses about this season of *The Real Housewives of Atlanta*—turns out he's a big fan and one of the women might be his great-great-great-great-grandniece—when Harriet abruptly interrupts us.

"Today I wanna talk about my first journey to freedom," she says, standing between Moses and me. Harriet inserts herself where she sees fit. She doesn't really ask permission. "That's what we need to work on next."

"Oh . . . okay," I say, while blinking my eyes and shaking my head as I quickly swig my Red Bull trying to keep up with her and her coffee. "Anything in particular you want to talk about in regards to your first journey?" I didn't expect to jump into the deep stuff so early, but maybe it's time to get into the nitty-gritty of what makes her story so remarkable.

She isn't answering me right away, though. Now I understand the meaning of the phrase "pregnant pause." She has already gone back to the pot to pour herself another cup of coffee and sits down with her back to me. Now I just feel silly. Feels like I'm on a date and I'm reading her signs all wrong. It's like I'm moving too fast.

"Let's go!" she barks at all of us. No one hesitates. I'm not gonna lie, this tiny little woman is very scary. She stands by the door waiting for us to file through one by one. As she moves you can see a glimpse of a wooden-handled pistol. This feels like it was done by design. I don't think she is going to shoot me, but I don't think she won't. We mobilize to go back to the rehearsal room. As we walk down that hall again she comes up from behind and passes all of us, taking the lead.

I whisper to Moses, "Is she mad at me?"

He talks to me under his breath. "No, this ain't got nothing to do with you. You just gotta understand that she done been down this road before. She used to have to tell her story over and over just to make money and help other Black folks. She did the whole abolitionist circuit." This was something I hadn't even considered, but now that I think about it, it makes sense.

When we make it back to the room Harriet makes sure she is the last to enter and she closes the door and locks it behind her. She starts pacing back and forth like she is gathering her thoughts. Everyone else just begins to set up their station, but Moses pulls me aside to continue our conversation.

"A lot of freed slaves and well-known abolitionists would travel around and tell their stories to raise money for the cause. Well-to-do abolitionists who didn't want to get their hands dirty would listen to people like Harriet, John Brown, Frederick Douglass, and Henry Box Brown talk about their journeys or about how they fought for freedom. When you consider how many people my sister persuaded to contribute to the abolitionist movement, there ain't no telling how many people she helped free." He says this with a lot of pride.

Moses is protective of Harriet, but he doesn't treat her delicately. He would be a fool to do so. That being said, she is a very complex woman. A minute ago she was sipping boiling-hot coffee like it was Gatorade on a hot summer day, now she is practically paralyzed with memories and emotion. As I embark on my own journey with Harriet and the Freemans, I wonder what I need freedom from. More than anything, I fear that I already know the answer and just don't want to admit it. Freedom is such a tricky concept. When are you really free? The question makes me think back to Nina Simone.

Moses turns his attention back to the *Housewives*. He's disappointed his niece, many times removed, threw a glass of champagne at one of her friends, though he understands why she did, but he's more impressed that she's done so well for herself. I almost show him her Instagram, but it's almost all ass shots so I decide against it.

"What about your people?" Moses asks me. "Where are you from?"

What a question. A really simple question. But I hadn't thought about it in a while, y'know? That means thinking about my mother, the only "people" I have left. She taught African American studies at a community college. She was very Afrocentric/new age Black power. I was the only kid at school in the nineties asking my lunch ladies if they had a vegan option. My mother didn't want me watching too much TV, I wasn't allowed to eat candy, and I sure as hell didn't listen to mainstream rap. She would always sit me down and tell me that freedom is earned, and you have to work to keep it. I was constantly reminded that Black people have to work twice as hard to get half the pay.

I got into a lot of trouble one day when my mother was waiting for me outside as the bus pulled up to drop me off from school. I chose to sit at the back of the bus with all the cool kids. You did not want to get caught sitting in the front next to the driver. That was lame. This was my first week at a new school and I didn't want them to know I was the weird vegan kid that had to eat my organic "Fruity Hoops" cereal with soy milk and wasn't allowed to listen to DMX. When the bus pulled up, my mother must've seen me get up from the back because she met me at the door, wearing a head wrap and a dress that looked like something Maya Angelou would wear in her later years. She wouldn't let me off the bus. I zipped up my winter coat and pulled my hoodie over my head to try and hide my face. I was so embarrassed. I already knew she was about to let me have it.

My mother climbed onto the bus and said, "Listen to me. I don't know about you all, but Darnell is not allowed to sit at the back of the bus!" Then she turned her anger toward me.

"Do you know how many Black people gave up their lives and freedom so that you could ride in the same seats as white people, and you have the nerve to choose to sit at the back of the bus? Ain't nothing cool about hanging out in the back and causing trouble."

I was so mortified I could barely move. I would have preferred a public beating. Anything would've been better than this. Then she turned back to the rest of the kids and gave the pièce de résistance. "And if any of you on this bus see him sitting in the back again, come knock on my door and I promise you he won't do it again."

She was very hard to understand when I was young, but as I got older all of it made sense. She just wanted me to enjoy and take pride in what we as a people had fought for. I understand that now. Every morning she used to drink coffee out of the same mug. It had a quote from Johann Wolfgang von Goethe printed on it: "NONE ARE MORE HOPELESSLY ENSLAVED THAN THOSE WHO FALSELY BELIEVE THEY ARE FREE." She would drink from this cup every morning across from me with the words facing me so I could read them clear as day. This is the kind of messaging that has stuck with me into adulthood, and it's moments like this that it all comes flooding back.

When Harriet paces past us, I use the opportunity to deflect Moses's question. "We don't have to talk about it today if you don't want to," I assure her.

"Oh no. We talking about it. You can bet your ass we

talking about it," she says, newly determined. "That's what we all came here to do, so we gon' talk and that's final!"

She has really put her tiny foot down, and I might've helped a little. Since she seems ready, we will dive right in. I don't want to waste any time.

"What made you decide to run? I imagine all slaves consider it, but what actually brings you to the decision to actually go through with it?"

She sits back in her chair with her arms folded. As if no one had ever bothered to ask her this particular question.

"We had a song we used to sing that really got deep in my soul."

OH, FREEDOM! OH, FREEDOM!
OH, FREEDOM OVER ME!
AND BEFORE I'D BE A SLAVE, I'LL BE BURIED IN MY GRAVE
AND GO HOME TO MY LORD AND BE FREE

She sings with her eyes closed and her fists clenched. She gets louder every time she repeats the chorus. She is leaned forward with her back hunched and you can see the veins popping in her neck as she gets louder and louder. The others start singing along with her, but with the acoustics of the room and the passion it sounds like I am listening to the Mississippi Mass Choir. The Freemans stop playing and sing the final phrase a cappella, sending shivers down my spine.

OH, FREEDOM! OH, FREEDOM!

OH, FREEDOM OVER ME!

AND BEFORE I'D BE A SLAVE, I'LL BE BURIED IN MY GRAVE

AND GO HOME TO MY LORD AND BE FREE

Harriet sits back and opens her eyes, now moist with tears. "This one of the songs we had to sing in private. This ain't the kind of song that you sang out in the field. If the white folks heard you singing this, you was sure to get a beating, or worse. After hearing this song so many times, one day it just solidified the feeling I already had in my heart. I had reasoned it out in my mind: There was one of two things I had the right to: liberty or death. If I could not have one, I would have the other. Running wasn't my first option, either. Hell, on paper I made a terrible runaway on account of the sleeping." She leans forward as she says this, with her elbows on her knees.

"I've heard about your condition," I admit. "I've read in books that you would often fall asleep for long periods of time. I imagine that would make it really hard to stay on the run."

She shot me a look like an auntie telling you to be quiet in church. "Well, do you want to tell my story or should I?"

I apologize and humbly step back, allowing her to continue.

When she was a young girl, she says, she was at a local grocer and the slave master was trying to discipline a young man who had run away. "He picked up a heavy floor weight, must've been about three or five pounds, and threw it at the young man's head. I'm sure you know by now that the weight done missed its intended target because that thing knocked my lights out. I got hit hard too. I don't even remember the story. I only know it because it's been told to me so many times."

Harriet wasn't sure she was going to make it after that, she could barely stand for months. "Let me tell you, a slave that can't work ain't long for this world, so I tried my best to keep working, but I wasn't doing much good. I think the only thing that saved my life was tha Lawd and my hair. You know I ain't never combed my hair a day in my life, and I do believe it saved me on that day." She takes a moment to rub her head as if she is feeling the pain all over again.

After that day, Harriet would just pass out right where she stood. But it wasn't a peaceful slumber. "I'm talking out cold in whatever position I collapsed into. That's if I wasn't having a shaking fit, but I did grow closer to the Lord." According to Harriet, she started to hear God's voice clearer than ever, she thinks due to her near-death experience. "From that day forward I never had a question about what tha Lawd was telling me."

Buck shifted in his seat in a very uncomfortable manner. We lock eyes only for a moment.

Her enslaver—I can't bring myself to call him her master—Edward Brodess, saw that she couldn't work and tried to sell Harriet, but nobody would buy her. "House slaves was supposed to be light-skinned and cute, plus I was injured so wasn't nobody trying to waste money on me," she explains. "Imagine that feeling. People coming around to look at you, then decide you ain't even worth the cheap-ass price they done put on you."

I can imagine it, but it makes my stomach turn with rage when I do. After praying every night for the Lord to change Brodess's heart, Harriet realized "it wasn't in his plan." So she decided to change her prayer. "I humbly asked tha Lawd to either change his heart or stop it so he could get out of my way. 'Bout a week or so later he died and that was all the sign I needed."

While I don't know if I believe in God, it's clear that Harriet Tubman has a spiritual connection with a higher power that seems to protect and guide her. It's a very compelling case for Christianity. Or just religion in general. It's comforting to believe in something greater than yourself, to believe that there's a greater plan for you. Comforting, if maybe, I don't know, naive. But it seems to work for Harriet, and I can't argue with that. "So he just fell over and died? Was it old age?"

"Naw, wasn't no old age. He wasn't nothing but about forty-seven. White folks live way longer than that. That was tha Lawd struck him down. He was standing in the way of my freedom and purpose."

Sometimes I hear stories like this and really start to wonder: What if there is a higher power looking out for us? Whether it's God or our ancestors or the universe itself. How do you explain away things that seem beyond explanation? Could it just be coincidence? But how many coincidences amount to a miracle? I guess it's just *easier* to believe in the unknowable.

"After Brodess died I knew they was about to start selling slaves to settle his debt and I wasn't about to sit around and wait my turn so me and two of my brothers tried to escape soon as we could," Harriet continues.

They had barely made it out of Maryland when her brothers got scared. They'd been on the run for about three weeks and, getting nervous, they turned back.

"I heard they was offering a hundred dollars for each one of us. It was mostly Ben who wanted to turn back. He was afraid of what they'd do to his son if he didn't turn back around. He was just hiding in the woods. We done run out of the food we was able to save up. I sure as hell didn't wanna turn back, but they made me. We was tired and hungry. Not getting much sleep 'cause we was nervous as all hell. We was able to come back without anyone noticing we was gone. The whole plantation was out of order because of the death of Brodess."

She still seems upset about it. I guess I would be too. To finally pursue freedom only to have to go back to being a slave. But they didn't know where they were going, Harriet explains.

"It ain't like slaves grow up looking at maps. I don't think you understand that. We had no clue where in the world we were. We didn't even know how big Maryland was, let alone how far away Pennsylvania was. It ain't like we had a notion of the lay of the land. Most of us had only ever seen the land we worked on and the land we'd been hired out to. We didn't have no concept of how long we was supposed to be running. It ain't like slaves escape and then come back to tell you how to do it. Well . . . not up until that point." She says this with a big smile on her face.

She's got a point. If I had to run away when the only world I had ever known was some shitty plantation in Maryland, I'd probably be dead within the week. You can tell Harriet's very proud of what she has accomplished—but in a very modest way, not in a boastful, unchristian way.

"That's really something to be proud of," I say to her.

"No, no, no. Ain't no glory in pride. I give all the glory to God. He the one done all this. I'm just the vehicle he used."

Somehow, I knew she would say that. The next time she decided she wasn't going to wait on her brothers. They were holding her back. Harriet knew she had a better chance of making it on her own. It hadn't even been a week when she tried her escape again.

"The last thing on earth you wanna be is a returned runaway," she said gravely. "I didn't have no interest in sticking around to see what they plans would be for me and my brothers if they ever found out we ran. I knew they wasn't gon' hurt us too bad 'cause they was still trying to sell us off, but still." I feel like she is still holding back. I want to know exactly what went on during that journey as she traveled north by herself.

"But how did you even know which way to go? I wouldn't even be able to make it here from my apartment without Google Maps."

She just stares at me blankly and asks, "What's a Google Map?"

I begin to explain but with no time for my shenanigans, she cuts me off. "No child, we wasn't using maps to navigate to the promised land. The songs helped me find my way to freedom. I know that when they said 'heaven' or 'the promised land' they was talking about anything north of the Mason-Dixon. When they said 'Jordan' or 'the River Jordan' they was talking about the Ohio River. I didn't even know that it wasn't called the River Jordan until I made it to Pennsylvania. But the most important song that helped so many people find freedom was 'Wade in the Water.' "

Even I know that one and start singing it, in spite of myself. I only know the first four lines but to my surprise Odessa joins me in harmony and Harriet just lets us sing together for a little bit. Once I have run out of lyrics, she continues.

"You learn to follow the river so dogs can't track you as easy, and you walk against the current 'cause the water flows south. The first time I traveled I just had to trust that all this was true. All I knew was I had seen people run and never return. I didn't know where they ended up, all I knew was it had to be better than where I was at the time."

It feels like we should take a break because she is starting to get teary-eyed. She seems to have too much dignity to wipe her eyes, but also too much dignity to let the tears fall. The tears are trapped in time with no way to escape.

"Do you wanna pause for a minute so you can gather yourself?" I ask as I get up to grab her a napkin. She reaches out and grabs my wrist with her tiny, skinny hand. She has a very strong and deliberate grip that stops me in my tracks.

"Something came over me when I got to freedom. I just knew I had reached the promised land. It was in this moment that I felt God's love stronger than I ever had before. My whole body felt different. When I found I had crossed that line, I looked at my hands to see if I was the same person. There was such a glory over everything; the sun came like gold through the trees and over the fields, and I felt like I was in heaven. I really felt like I was in heaven. I don't even know that I can explain the feeling to someone who ain't never been a slave. Best way I can say it is: You finally feel like yourself." She is now staring straight into my eyes and I can tell she knows she is speaking directly to my soul. She is looking way past my physical form and is connecting with me on a molecular level. I can feel the hot tears begin to sting my eyes.

She continues, "I had crossed the line. I was free, but there was no one to welcome me to the land of freedom. I was a stranger in a strange land, and my home after all was down in Maryland, because my father, my mother, my brothers, and sisters were there. But I was free . . . and they should have been free. I hadn't even been free for a whole minute and I already knew tha Lawd had work for me to do."

For just a moment we feel like the same person and her grip has not loosened even a little bit. I try to release my wrist to wipe a tear from my eye but she won't let go. "Let it go, baby."

Without warning, my body breaks down. I can't stop myself from crying. This is not pretty television crying. This is the type of crying where you can't catch your breath and you've abandoned any sense of vanity. All I can do is fall into her arms and thank her a thousand times. It becomes clearer than ever that I wouldn't have any of the freedoms I have if this woman hadn't sacrificed everything for people who were once in the same situation she had been born into. When all the cards seemed to be stacked against her, she still rose to the occasion. She is Black, illiterate, handicapped, born a slave, tiny, completely plain looking, and yet she saw something special in herself. But it's hard to deny. Everyone who meets Harriet sees it, too. As she holds me she sings to me:

OH, FREEDOM! OH, FREEDOM!

OH, FREEDOM OVER ME!

AND BEFORE I'D BE A SLAVE

I'LL BE BURIED IN MY GRAVE

AND GO HOME TO MY LORD AND BE FREE

OH, FREEDOM! OH, FREEDOM!

OH, FREEDOM OVER ME!

AND BEFORE I'D BE A SLAVE

I'LL BE BURIED IN MY GRAVE

CHAPTER 5

NOW THAT MOST OF US HAVE seen ourselves reduced to tears I think the sugarcoating on our acquaintance has officially been licked off. Watching someone break down and cry is completely intimate. In many ways it's more intimate than sex. It feels like everyone here has seen me in my underwear, and not the nice ones. I'm talking "laundry day" underwear.

The best part is, I don't feel judged. In fact, I feel closer if anything. You know when you go to summer camp and at the end of every summer you are convinced these are the most important people in your life? That's where I am at this moment.

And for all intents and purposes they are the most important people in my life. Putting this album and show together is the most important thing I have going for me right now, and I don't think I'll be admitting that out loud at any point.

It's the next day and I'm in the car headed to the studio. I'm a little nervous to see everyone, but I know that I have nothing to worry about. I still feel very ostracized by the music industry and by my former friends so I don't have a lot of people in my life right now.

As I get out of my car I grab some muffins and a carton of coffee. I hope they don't mind the vegan muffins. I know Quakes won't. But just to be safe, I don't think I'm going to tell them. I walk into the reception room and everyone is standing in a circle looking at the floor. I assume they are praying so I do the tiptoe you do in church.

"She gon' be like this for a while," Moses tells me as he turns around to grab some of the muffins I have laid out.

As he moves I realize that Harriet is contorted on the floor. It really doesn't look comfortable. I rush in to try and help her but Buck is already leaning her on her side.

"Should we call an ambulance or something?"

"Naw, we just lean her on her side and wait till she wake up. She'll be all right," Buck assures me. "This happens all the time."

Everyone seems so calm about it. It looks like she fainted. I've heard it described as narcolepsy, but this doesn't look like sleeping. She looks like she has been knocked unconscious. If they didn't seem so calm I'd put a mirror under her nose to make sure she was breathing.

"So what do we do now?" I ask the room. It naturally feels like Odessa is second in command here, so I turn my attention to her.

"Don't look at me. You the conductor now." That's when I realize everyone else is looking at me.

"Let's all just take a break," I say, not knowing what else to do. I join Moses over by the coffee. It's way too early for me to be in charge without even an ounce of caffeine in my system. "That's really scary," I say to him.

"You get used to it. She ain't in pain. She ain't in trouble. She probably gon' come to telling us about how she communed with God. This happened when we was kids, and it even happened when we was running, too. Now *that* was scary, 'cause she was the only one who knew the way," he says as he blows on his coffee and takes a sip. He does not drink coffee like Harriett. Moses is much more relatable.

I don't feel intimidated by him. When I compare myself to Harriet, I can really start to feel like I am underperforming, but Moses is more of an everyman. If Harriet is "goals," then Moses is "relatable content," and that is a welcome contrast.

Still, for how superhuman Harriet is, she looks so

vulnerable over there, contorted in the corner, frozen in fright. It must have fallen on Moses, more than anybody, to take care of her. I wonder what she did when she was all alone. Was she scared? How did she avoid getting caught when she couldn't control if and when she would suddenly pass out? But Harriet is in no position to answer any of my questions, so I try Moses instead.

"When did you first hear that she was coming back for you?"

"Well, I knew she was gon' come back for me at some point. I just didn't know when," he says, looking at me in a way that both unsettles and excites me.

I look down and then back at Harriet.

"It's kind of ironic that they started calling her Moses."

"*Did* that ever get confusing?" I ask him. "You both being called Moses?"

"All the time. Confusing. And annoying. I started hearing tell of Moses setting all the slaves free, and I didn't want the Brodess family to think I had anything to do with it."

"Did they ever suspect anything? The Brodesses?"

"Nah. I really think . . ." He looks over his shoulder to make sure no one else can hear us—he seems especially concerned about Quakes. "I think white folks just see what they wanna see. It's like they in denial about shit."

This is the first time I've heard him swear, or say anything of that nature for that matter. He seems to be a little more himself when Harriet isn't around. Maybe there is still a lot of that big-sister energy over him, even after all these centuries.

"You'd have thought they woulda noticed after Harriet and my brothers escape the first time. Then they return and Harriet escape again. Then she come back and free damn near the whole family. She had already got my brothers and my parents so I knew she wouldn't leave me."

I look over again at Harriet and marvel that this comatose woman could have done all that. And I realize that we have more in common than I thought. I'm paralyzed, too, stuck in one position. The only difference is, Harriet eventually wakes up from her stupor. I've been in mine for nearly twenty years.

I can't even imagine the patience it must take to wait your turn for freedom. Hell, I don't even like to sit through commercials on YouTube. "What was it like when Harriet finally came for you?"

He gives me that look again but this time I refuse to look away. In his eyes, I can almost see what he's telling me. "Whenever you would hear the song 'Sweet Chariot,' you would get such a chill in your bones 'cause you knew Harriet was nearby to help more people. Maybe this was your day. This was her favorite song to sing. When somebody would hear her singing it faintly from the woods they would start to sing it right away, so that the white folks and Uncle Toms wouldn't know where it was coming from. That song just meant that this was somebody's last night in bondage."

Out of instinct, I gather everyone around. Harriet wouldn't want us to just be sitting there, dawdling, while she was out cold. I tell them to play "Swing Low, Sweet Chariot," and invite Moses to start talking over it, as Harriet had done. He is shy at first, but he relents. The call of the spotlight is undeniable for someone who's always been just to the side of it his whole life.

"A lot of the time it was the pastor who would deliver the news to us," Moses begins, hesitant but quickly growing in confidence. "White folks would go easier on the preachers than they would with other slaves because they used to use the preacher to keep us in line . . . or so they thought. The preacher would say that he was walking in the nearby woods to commune with the Lord and the white folks would never question it because he always came back. The biggest disservice they ever did to their own cause was convincing themselves that we was stupid." Moses has a big grin on his face thinking about all the times they outsmarted the slavers.

"Was it the preacher who gave you the news?"

"Sure was. The preacher came to me in the field and told me to come see him in the night. We had a run-down little shack they called a church for us. He just came up to me and says, 'Moses, let me pray for you tonight.' I knew what that meant. Soon as he said it, I think I almost passed out, but I had to keep it together. Didn't want none of the slavers to understand what was going on. It was important not to ever reveal the code, 'cause somebody after is still gon' have to use it."

I start taking notes about how to turn this into a song, but I want Moses to keep going. "I can't even imagine what that must be like," I prod him. "You're being told you're about to be free and you're about to see your sister."

"Now, I still didn't know who Moses was. I assumed it was Harriet, but only the preacher knew for sure. And that man can keep a secret. Everybody trusted him. He was one of the most noble out of everybody. He didn't escape until we was freed by Lincoln. He stayed behind on purpose to help out as many folks as he could. A lot of folks did that. They whole mission was to stay behind and make a way. They was in the most danger out of everybody. Catching a runaway was one thing, but helping one . . . oh, your days was numbered. If you get caught helping you might as well get ready to go on to glory." He shudders at the thought. He grabs his coffee, blowing on it still, even though there's no way it's hot by this point.

The band stops playing and I start pacing like Harriet did

yesterday. Moses's story is so inspiring I have all these ideas running through my head, hooks and beats and melodies that I want to get down immediately. I open my laptop and start producing. It's like I can *see* Harriet singing in the woods. I can see Moses . . . What is Moses doing? I stop and look up at him. "Moses, how did you prepare to run?"

He scoffs. "Prepare? Ain't nothing to prepare. It ain't like you moving down the street. You about to leave home and never come back. You don't know what to get ready for. You don't know how long you gon' be traveling. You hear the phrase "head up north," but you don't even have a concept of what north is. I remember the first time I saw a map. I felt so small. Felt like the first time I realized how big the world was. Made me feel good though." He has become a little fidgety. His shyness is taking over again. I can see him shift his body language.

I try to bring him back. "So what did you do when you finally saw your sister?"

He's holding his cup with both hands, looking at the floor. "You ain't never seen nothing that beautiful. She finally look how she supposed to look. Something about her different. Her whole attitude and look done changed. She look important and strong. Not scared and sheepish. I almost didn't recognize her. We can't make no noise so we just hold each other in silence for a few minutes. There ain't a whole lot of time to linger, so we head to the woods. It all happened so fast I couldn't even appreciate it."

In my time with Harriet and the Freemans I have learned about how brilliant, resilient, and innovative Black people, my people, are. Without knowledge of how to read or write, without any method of communication besides word of mouth, without rights, without freedom—hell, without even being allowed to make eye contact in some cases, they were able to engineer a system of communication so complex and intricate that not even the slickest of slave catchers could decode it. The methods used by runaways were such a safely guarded secret, yet the information always got to the person who needed to hear it.

The others seem to be milling about minding their business. Every so often Odessa would walk over to Harriet to quickly check on her.

"Is she okay?" I ask her.

"I think so. It's not as scary when we ain't on the run. When she pass out on a trip north you be so scared you don't know what to do." She pulls up a chair to sit near Harriet. "Imagine having the most famous fugitive in America passed out in your home and you don't have the strength to move her."

"The slavers did not like us Quakers, so they were constantly keeping an eye on us," Quakes chimes in. "Many of us used our homes to help runaways and other conductors. But you could not use your house as a safe place too many times in a row."

"What about the trips headed back south? I assume she made these trips alone?" I look over at Harriet's limp body still rolled on her side and think about her alone in the woods by the riverside completely passed out.

"She didn't always go back by herself although she would a lot of the time," Odessa says, stroking Harriet's forehead. "Sometimes people would accompany her on the route, maybe even just for a day or two. The Underground Railroad wasn't all in the woods, or actually underground. Some of it was on public streets and in plain sight."

"That's the part that makes it so genius," Buck says. Suddenly, we're all gathered around Harriet. "They thought Harriet was a member of several communities, because she came around so often. And she moved a lot faster by herself. Normally she didn't have that many people with her. She couldn't do the trips back-to-back, because she had to raise money to travel."

"Now, my sister wasn't the only conductor on the Underground Railroad, but she was for sure the best and most famous," Moses adds, and I understand what he's getting at. I mean sure, Beyoncé wasn't the only member of Destiny's Child but . . . you get my drift. The Beyoncé of the

Railroad . . . Is that a song? No . . . maybe. I'll make a note just in case.

"Most people didn't even know she was a woman," Buck says. "Some people even thought she was a spirit. There just ain't no way one person can make that many trips and never get caught."

"It sure wasn't for a lack of effort on the slave catchers' part neither," Odessa adds in. "They was looking high and low for her and couldn't come up with nothing."

"They was actually offering a hundred dollars each for her and my brothers!" Moses says with a laugh. "I ain't never seen that kind of money in my life. I know Negroes that would've turned theyselves in for that much money." I open my phone and do the math.

"That would be about ten thousand today," I tell Moses.

"Ten thousand dollars!" He raises his eyebrows. "I ain't never seen *that much money* in my life."

Buck seems less impressed. "That was the kind of money that turned Blacks on each other. A lot of the slave catchers was Black folks. They would use Black people because they could get more information than whites could. Even free Black people didn't trust white folks. You would only tell a white person something private if you absolutely had to. That could backfire on you real quick, 'cause a lot of them didn't even see us as human. Our lives didn't mean nothing to them. You know how degrading it is to listen to someone promise you to they children? Like you a family heirloom or something." He shakes his head in disgust.

"Did that happen a lot?" I ask.

"All the time," Buck says. "The worst was when they promised to free you after they death or by a certain age. It was so awful 'cause they rarely did it. By the time you old and you waiting on that day they always come up with an excuse."

"Usually white folks didn't bother no Black preachers," Moses interjects. "I think that's because most of the time they was preaching to us to honor our masters and be subservient. Some of the preachers believed it, and others were doing that as a front, because they knew if they told us that Jesus loved us, and that we deserved freedom, we would rise up." An expression flashes across Moses's face as he says, "It's funny to me how they always skipped over the story of Moses when talking about Bible stories."

Funny, sure. The story of a man, following the will of God, freeing the slaves and punishing their enslavers. What could go wrong with that?

"We often got information from the Black preacher in town," Moses continues. "Sometimes we would hide in the church the night before our escape. That's what I did. There was a few of us, mostly families. I tell you your heart is racing and you scared."

"Not just scared," Odessa adds. "You excited, hopeful, and full of dread at the same time. You ain't never not been under the eye of a white man with a whip. When you leave the grounds for the first time you know there ain't no turning back. If you on a trip with Moses you sees it till the end, and that sure as hell ain't up for debate."

Buck tells the story of a man who said he was scared and wanted to turn around. "Boy, I tell you he said the wrong thing. Pretty soon he found himself looking down the business end of a pistol with Harriet attached to it."

"That's the thing," Moses says, taking up the thread. "When you get on board with the conductor she tells you before you even take a single step: 'If you tired, keep going. If you scared, keep going. If you hungry, keep going. If you want to taste freedom, keep going. And if you try and turn around and go back, I will shoot you where you stand. You'll be lucky to get one step in the opposite direction and I'm harder to get away from than any slave catcher.' "

"I reckon most of the folks would rather die than go back to slavery," Buck says.

"A few just got a little cold in the feet," Odessa manages to get in before Moses, once again free of his shyness, finishes the tale of the would-be deserter.

"Harriet must've had the same look in her eye that night that my momma had when the white folks came and tried to take me, 'cause that man turned right back around and continued his journey. She knew that if anyone made it back to the plantation it could compromise not only the people who had escaped and everyone who had helped us on the way, but anybody that would've had a chance after us."

I am glaring out into space, causing Moses to pause, as if I'm judging Harriet's actions. "She didn't do it to be mean," he says, "she did it because . . . "

"I did it 'cause it was necessary," Harriet says, rubbing her eyes. She looks completely disheveled. Her face is puffy, her eyes completely red, and her headscarf has fallen off, exposing her hair, which is completely matted. Buck walks her over to a chair and brings her coffee, but she doesn't seem interested in drinking it.

"Sometimes it takes me a while to gather myself after I've been out."

I don't know how long she's been awake and I'm not sure how much of that she heard. I imagine that by this point in her life she's used to hearing people talk about her like she's not in the room. She rubs her head as if she's nursing a headache that she can't seem to best.

"Is there anything I can do for you?" I ask her. It's clear I'm the only one in the room that hasn't been in this situation yet.

"I wanna know what you gonna do for yourself," she

says, staring daggers through my head. I have no clue what she is talking about so I let out an uncomfortable laugh while looking around the room to see how everyone else is taking this in.

"What do you mean?"

"I'm in the business of taking people to freedom and you ain't free from something. Now what it is I don't know and that ain't none of my business." She slowly stands up. "But we gon' get you to the promised land."

CHAPTER 6

HARRIET OFTEN WORKS IN PARABLES. BUT this one is completely lost on me. The promised land? Is she trying to convert me? I have no qualms with being the center of attention, but everyone is looking directly at me and I feel very uncomfortable. I feel like they expect me to say or do something. I have nothing to offer them right now.

"What?" I ask the room. I can admit that I am being a little defensive. Everyone just looks back at me awkwardly.

No one is responding so I walk over to the watercooler and pour Harriet a glass of water, but she has already stomped her way over to the carton of coffee, having already drained the cup Buck poured for her earlier. I don't think the coffee will actually make her feel better, but she seems pretty sure of what she wants.

Handing her the glass that I only filled halfway I ask, "What do you mean by that?"

She takes a little sip of coffee. Then she finishes it off and takes the cup of water out of my hand and drinks it all in one gulp. I think she wants more water so I go get it without waiting for her to ask.

"Whenever I pass out I don't ever come back empty-handed. That's when tha Lawd talks to me the loudest. See, Darnell, I ain't nothing but a vessel doing tha Lawd's work. Ain't none of this plan mine." She just glares at me. I don't get what she's hinting at.

"Did he say anything about me?" I laugh out loud. She doesn't even crack a smile.

"Let's just say he showed me the safest way to get to where I'm headed, and I ain't going alone." She hands the glass back to me and gestures over to the watercooler as if she would like more water.

I return with the glass, full this time, and she takes it out of my hand before I even extend it to her, drinking the whole glass while maintaining eye contact with me. She's starting to scare me.

"Thank you," she says with very heavy breath and just a little water dribbling down her chin. "I get so thirsty some-times." She grabs a handkerchief and dabs her chin. We both sit in silence for a moment, but it isn't awkward. It feels like we've earned it.

"I know that we've been going over a lot here," I tell Harriet. "I can imagine it's very stressful to have to—" She cuts me off.

"I really don't mind talking to people about my life, 'cause I know I'm serving a greater purpose. All the abolitionists, especially the Black ones, are used to talking about our struggles. We used to go up in front of dozens, sometimes hundreds of people preaching the word of abolition."

It looks like she is thinking fondly of these times. For some reason I assumed she'd be anguished at the thought of having to relive moments from her time as a slave or as a conductor.

"It doesn't upset you at all?" I ask her.

"Now I ain't say that," she says, instantly snapping herself out of the past. "It do take a lot out of me to talk about my life, but it would take even more if I didn't." She never seems to be done with her work. Even though she is no longer taking trips, she is still willing to go back for people who may be left behind. It's hard not to compare yourself to her. And feel completely inadequate.

"Usually the other abolitionists would gather in a church or a raggedy little tent. Different abolitionists would get all the people together. One of my favorites was John Brown. You know 'bout John Brown?" she asks me. I had to rack my brain to remember.

"I think I may have heard of him, but to be honest I don't remember much. Was he a former slave, too?"

"He was a crazy old white man!" Odessa yells from across the room.

"That he was," Harriet says, shaking her head. "But he had a good heart. I heard about him through my underground connections. A lot of the conductors was scared of him, and for good reason, too. The man would ask you if you was pro slavery or free states and if you said the wrong answer you better hope you sounded good saying it, 'cause those would've been your last earthly words. He was nutty as squirrel turd, but ever since the day I met him he treated me with nothing but respect. Nutty as he was, he was a gentleman. I ain't never had a white man talk to me the way John Brown did. Not even in Canada. He the reason they call me 'General' Tubman." She has a huge smile on her face.

"Everybody was afraid of John Brown, but when I met with him I wasn't even a little nervous. I was excited. I heard he was a man of faith so I knew tha Lawd would keep me safe while I was with him. Plus, when I first met him he took his hat off." She pauses with her mouth open, still in shock. I guess the sentiment is lost on me.

"Clearly some folks wasn't born slaves in the 1800s and it shows," Odessa remarks with a side-eye.

"White folks didn't treat Black folks with no amount of respect back then," Moses explains. "Not even in the North."

"The historians would have you believe that once you crossed the Pennsylvania state line, white folks start bowing to you and start inviting you to their fancy lunch parties," Harriet says, without a hint of bitterness. "Lawd knows that ain't the case. But the way John Brown respected me gave others the idea I should be respected, too."

This makes me think of every interaction I've ever had with a white person to this day. Did they treat me with the utmost respect, and how would they have treated me in 1855? What was the last fancy white lunch party I was invited to? I'm finding it harder and harder to imagine what life could have been like for them—Harriet, Moses, Odessa, all of them—because it's so far removed from my own experience. Like Odessa said, I wasn't born a slave in the 1800s. And it shows. Just then I get an idea.

"Ms. Tub— Harri— Minty, I want to go somewhere with you. With all of you . . . " I'm hesitant to even bring it up, but this studio isn't doing my imagination any favors.

"Well." Harriet stares at me impatiently. I'm taking too long to get out the words.

"I— I want to see where you were born."

"This nigga!" says Buck, who until now was silently lurking in the corner.

"Hush!" Harriet tells him, and that building of a man pipes down with quickness. "Now why on God's green earth would you want to go back there?"

"Well . . . " I begin, but before I can convince myself of the words I'm about to say, I hear Moses.

"I think it's a good idea," he says, shooting me a glance.

"Who asked you?" Harriet tells more than asks him, the big sister in her written all over her face.

"The boy's been living in an urban jungle," Moses says, standing his ground. "What does he know of a slave's life? Wouldn't hurt to give him firsthand experience."

"You ready to be in chains, boy?" Buck taunts me.

"I didn't mean that, just—"

"Hush! Both of yous!"

Moses and Buck immediately clam up as Harriet fixes me with a stare, as if determining what it is I'm playing at exactly. "Okay," she says finally.

"Okay?" I can't really believe she agreed to it. After all, who would want to go back to where they were born into bondage? I have a hard time just going back home to visit my mother.

"I said okay. Let's go."

"Right now?"

"Yes, right now. If we start walking now, we'll get there in, oh, about, five days, four if we really step on it." Harriet then starts getting ready to leave, and the Freemans all follow suit and they're damn near halfway out the door before I can stop them.

"Wait, wait, I can just rent a van. We don't have to walk," I tell Harriet, who stops, then squints at me in disbelief.

"Woo, Lawd!" Odessa exhales. "That's a relief. I've done all the walking I care to do in my lifetime. I sure do love living in the *twenty-first* century."

Harriet starts to grumble something about "that racist ass Henry Ford" and I start looking up van rentals because I guess we're doing this.

· · ·

An hour later, we're all stuffed into a 2005 minivan, Harriet riding shotgun, with everyone else in the back. Harriet starts in again on her beloved crazy old white man.

"John Brown had a beard that was all the way down to his nipples," Harriet tells me as we enter Pennsylvania. "And he sure didn't like to take care of it. He looked a shabby ole mess with food always stuck in it. For a man so skinny he was always eating something. I ain't never seen him without that ratty old beard, but I heard that without it he looked like an ugly version of Abraham Lincoln, and let's just say Lincoln was not known for his looks." She lets out a belly laugh that infects the whole van and suddenly we're all laughing.

Quakes is burning a fat joint in the back and passing it between himself, Buck, and Moses, as Odessa complains about the smell and the smoke. Harriet, however, doesn't seem to mind but she doesn't ever partake. But when I start coughing heavily from the smoke, she grabs the joint out of my hand and passes it back to Buck.

"Keep your eyes on the road! I don't trust these contraptions," she says, referring to the van. Even though it's an old model, it still pretty much drives itself, but Harriet is not someone you argue with.

"What happened between you and John Brown?" I ask, hoping to pass the time with a couple more hours left in our trip.

She perks right up.

"Chile, I feel bad for that man. He sure wasn't lacking in ambition I'll tell you that. But he might have fallen a little short in execution and paying attention to the details. He was so focused on the big picture that he forgot about all the little stuff. His ideas were great but he could rarely pull off what he was aiming for. Plus, I ain't never met a single person that was as lucky and unlucky as John Brown. He the kind of man that would dodge a hundred bullets in a battle, then trip and break his leg after the victory."

She shakes her head like she still feels sorry for him. "He really believed in putting guns in the hands of every slave in the South. That's when he really got the slavers scared. Some abolitionists wanted to free Blacks, but John Brown wanted to help us get revenge. He really believed in an eye for an eye. He thought that the vengeance of tha Lawd was his to exact. He felt he was the executioner of God's will, and by his standards he did just that. There was a time when he was the most feared man in America. Most abolitionists were nonviolent. Just helping people escape by sneaking around, but that wasn't enough for John. John Brown wanted blood in the streets."

It's getting dark and I realize I hadn't really thought out this trip. Are we going to stay over in Maryland? I start looking for rest stops along the road.

"His small battalion was hodgepodge as all hell," Harriet continues. "It was one thing to see Blacks and whites mixing, but he had Indians, Blacks, whites, even a few mulattos that could pass for either white or Black. He had children and even a few women in his group. They was every bit as committed as he was. To be a part of his group you had to be. One of his soldiers found me in Gettysburg and told me that John Brown was planning something big and that he needed help from me, the General.

"No one knows the backwoods of Dorchester County

like I do, and if anyone knows a group of people that was to cut the head off the ugly snake called slavery, it's me. So, I agreed to help him. I told them where to meet me and when to meet me. They call me the Conductor 'cause I ain't never late."

The General. The Conductor. Moses. Harriet Tubman has more nicknames than Lil Wayne.

"If I tell you I'm coming to pick you up, you best believe I'll see you there," Weezy F. Tubman says. "I had to gather my men and spread the word so I needed a few months. When I finally got my group and plan together I set out to meet up with John. He never showed up. I never saw or heard from him again."

Harriet is silent for a while but now I actually want to know more about John Brown after she volunteered all this information about him and his nipple-grazing beard. "What happened to him?" I ask impatiently.

Harriet shrugs. "All I know is that it didn't end well for John Brown. He gave the effort everything he had, including his life and the life of two of his boys, to fight for the likes of me and my people. I really think his death was what caused the Civil War. He went into the belly of the beast. He didn't make it out, but the beast had an upset stomach from that day forward." She goes silent again and then, talking to no one in particular, she says, "You stick around long enough

and you gon' have a lot of people to miss. Trust me on that."
She finishes and takes a deep breath.

Harriet just stares out the window as the passing power
lines and billboards are replaced by trees the deeper we get
into the country. The sun will set soon and I'd rather not be
stuck out here. It's time to find a place to stay for the night.
I see a sign for a motel and I'm thankful that all six-foot-
something of Buck is with us, hunched over in the third row
all by himself since no one else could, or wanted to, fit next
to him.

We pull into the motel lot, one of those fancy numbers
with a communal toilet. But it's the only place around for
miles so I guess this is where we're staying. I pull out my
wallet and head to the front desk, but before I can put one
foot in front of the other, Harriet pushes me out of the way
and pulls out a large stack of twenty-dollar bills, all with her
face on them. "A little gift from Uncle Sam," she tells me with
a wink. She takes one of the bills, holds it up, and remarks,
"Not a bad likeness." Then she makes a beeline for the little
office tucked away under a flight of stairs.

A few minutes later she comes stomping out with a few
keys. Everyone has their own room except me and Harriet.
We're sharing a room with two hard, starchy double beds
and no TV.

Everyone has probably gone to bed but Harriet is still up

and pacing. Having run so much in her life she must find it impossible to stop, to just sit still. I close my eyes to try and rest but I can only hear Harriet's uneven footsteps against the dusty carpet.

"Did you ever see John Brown again?" I ask her, thinking it might calm her.

She stops and stares at me with a hint of amusement. "Boy, I thought most Black folks could read today. You ain't never picked up a history book? He didn't make it out of Harpers Ferry a free man, and they sure wasn't offering no visitation in the days before he was s'posed to see the hangman."

"He was hanged?" I ask in shock.

"Of course he was hanged! You gotta remember, this was before the Civil War. John Brown terrified slavers and Southerners. The only thing that scares a racist white man more than a smart Black woman fighting for her freedom is the white man that helps her."

She goes on and on about John Brown for what feels like another thirty minutes, which is way longer than you think it is in real time. She keeps talking about how poorly he planned, and how the few times she did see him what a mess he was, but that she was impressed with how everyone respected him. They were most likely all afraid of him. "He was a crazy old white man with a gun and a reputation for shooting and asking questions after. When someone feels justified by tha Lawd it's really hard to try and talk them down. When you feel like you are doing tha Lawd's work there is nothing an earthly being can say to change your mind."

It's clear that she misses John Brown and wishes things had turned out differently for him. "After everything you've been through, I assume you would avoid white people at all costs," I say to her.

"Well, I sure as hell ain't seeking them out, I can tell you that," she says with a half-hearted laugh. "It ain't even about avoiding white people, though. The reason we was going around to all the rallies and meetings in churches and tents was because people can't do better if they don't know better. We knew we had to tell our stories. Plus, Black folks can't sit here and end racism and slavery in America. This is a white folks problem. White folks the ones that created this system and they gon' have to take part in its undoing."

But what if, to this day, there are more white folks willing to keep the system intact than those willing to take it apart? Harriet believes in people, in the good in people. After all she's been through, she still believes people can change.

"Keeping Black folks oppressed is only half the battle," she continues, sitting on the edge of her bed. "The richest of white folks have also convinced the poorest of white folks that if Blacks was to become equal, if Black folks got rights, if Black folks was seen on the same level as white folks, that it would somehow be bad for them." She says this while clutching her headscarf in her hand.

"The folks that could afford slaves were sure as hell not fighting in the war. Instead, it was poor and uneducated white people, and Blacks being convinced or forced by the ones with all the money. You gotta keep folks ignorant if you wanna control them. That's why they didn't want us reading or writing."

My sleepy eyes widen. "What about Black folks that could read, like Frederick Douglass?"

"Lord, you obsessed with that man," she says, flicking her wrist at me. "And you ain't the only one, either. You know he was the most photographed Negro in the world at the time. White folks loved taking pictures of him. He was handsome, too. Black men didn't come more dignified than Frederick Douglass, and he was real-life famous too. Was well known, when you really didn't wanna be. The very first time I heard him talk I couldn't even believe I was hearing the words of a former slave. He talked like a white man with a expensive education. That's why some Black folks didn't like him. Thought he was uppity, but that some backwards-ass thinking that white folks done put in our head." She says this with a lot of venom, then stands and starts pacing again.

"They got us thinking we only supposed to be seen in

one way." She seems more awake now. "Got us thinking that we not supposed to believe in ourselves, or know big words. So that way when you see another Black person doing all the things you feel you ain't supposed to do, you call him a uppity nigger just like white folks do. I liked him, though. He even wrote me a real nice letter one time."

I sit up with a start in my bed. "Wait! You met Frederick Douglass?" I must sound like an excited schoolboy.

"Don't have a damn conniption. Of course I met him. Didn't I tell you all the abolitionists knew each other?" she says to me.

"Are you sure it was him?"

"Yeah. I'm sure," she says, slightly annoyed. "He ain't somebody you mistake for another. For a colored man he dressed like he was damn near made of money, he talked like he went to school with white folks, and he had that hair. Everybody knew that hair. He got to talk to presidents, went overseas, he done earned the respect of all these white folks because they was intimidated by him. They didn't know a Black man could be that smart. And I mean book smart. He came from slavery to being known as one of the smartest people in America. Imagine that, would you? He ain't go to college, he taught hisself how to read. Not just taught hisself, but other slaves too. He done ran away twice. That's what I mean when I talk about how strong Black folks are. From shackles to shaking hands with the president of the United States in one lifetime. That's why every time I take somebody with me I say, 'We gon' make it to the promised land,' 'cause I know we can make it."

I am now fully awake, my eyes starting to gleam in the light of the lamp on the end table. Maybe it's not that Harriet can't rest but that she sees no need for it.

"We wasn't made to break, or snap, or fall apart," she says, talking to me as if she's preaching to a crowd of hundreds. "We made out of something stronger than steel and diamonds combined. I can't stand when I see folks say they can't make it. I just look at them and say, 'Baby, do you know where you come from? Do you know what you made of? Do you know who your ancestors are? Do you have any idea what you are capable of?' "

Harriet pauses, then grabs my hand and clenches it tight. "Now I want you to take yo time with me, 'cause I'm gon' take my time with you. Remember we on the road to freedom now, and we don't turn back."

I feel an odd combination of uncomfortable and completely loved. It feels like she is affording me a love that I haven't been kind enough to extend to myself. Maybe I have some past trauma that makes me want to take up as little space as possible. There have been times when I made the decision to be myself and claim my space and it backfired in the moment. I tend to minimize myself even when people tell me I don't have to. I'm making a conscious effort to stop doing that.

"What's the matter?" she asks me. We are still holding hands and I don't want her to let go so I grab her other hand.

"Thank you," is all I can think to say.

CHAPTER 7

THE NEXT MORNING, EVERYONE SEEMS READY to blow this dicey motel, except Harriet, who strolls out of our room fresh as a daisy.

"Good morning, y'all," she says, piping-hot coffee in hand and doing a little energetic strut over to Buck, Moses, Quakes, Odessa, and me standing impatiently by the van.

"Somebody is in a good mood," I say as she hums a little tune. She glances at me through the steam of her coffee.

"Baby, I'm happy more often than you think. I ain't always smiling, but that don't mean I'm mad all the time," she says while taking little breaks to blow on her coffee. "The question should be: How come you ain't as happy as me?"

This woman really has a way of reading me to filth. But in a loving way that leaves me speechless. We pile into the minivan, everyone happy to be rid of this joint, and I floor it out of there. When the motel is finally out of sight from the rearview mirror, I see my chance.

"We gotta talk about the war," I say, nervous that this might not be the best subject to start the day. "I don't want to dive in headfirst with no regard for your feelings, but I also don't want to tiptoe around it either."

Buck and Moses look at each other, pause for a moment, and let out a belly laugh at the exact same time that shakes the entire van. I really don't see what's so funny. I've been crafting this sentence since I woke up this morning. I thought it'd be like dropping a hydrogen bomb on a trailer park, but it was received more like a fart joke in a kindergarten class. "What's so funny?" I ask with a straight face. Buck is trying to ease his laughter.

"It's just how serious you looked when you said it. You really thought you was laying the law down or something."

Buck and Moses start to laugh again, Moses turning around in his seat to face Buck as they exchange playful slaps with each other.

"Y'all stop it now," Odessa says. "He was just trying to show some compassion."

"At least you know they like you," Quakes says, suppressing a chuckle. It's a weird way to show it but I believe him.

"Well, it feels like they're laughing at me," I say.

"Because we are!" Moses says, which ignites another burst of laughter, this time from everyone, including Harriet. Odessa is trying her best to cover her mouth so I can't see her laughing. Even I have to admit that was kind of funny.

"I will pull this car over right now!" I say, half joking.

Harriet calms the ruckus in the van, perhaps afraid I might drive us off a cliff or something. "They just laughing 'cause they done been through this a thousand times," she explains. "If you ain't telling the story to some white person with a pen and pad, then you telling it to people who wasn't even alive to remember. You ain't wrong about approaching it like that, though. It's a sore spot for a lot of people. Talk to me if you wanna know something. I ain't gon' laugh at ya."

The air in the minivan is once again sober. Harriet, the Conductor, has the thankless task of keeping us on track. We drive the hour to Brodess Farm in near silence. Or maybe we're all aware of the weight of returning to what was essentially a prison for some of them. And so I feel kinda shitty when we finally pull up to the farm and I'm . . . disappointed. It's just . . . land. Wide, open, serene, with a tiny, abandoned church the only thing left standing.

Harriet is silent for a great while staring off into the distance, possibly remembering what happened here almost two centuries ago. Moses goes off to wander the grounds, with Buck and the others following loosely behind. Harriet wanders over to a sign and asks me to read it to her. She never did learn to read or write.

"Harriet Tubman, 1820–1913," I read. She lived to ninety-three years old! She looks anywhere between forty and seventy, but ninety-three could be possible. She's got that Cicely Tyson kind of aged but ageless face. I keep reading, "The 'Moses of her people,' Harriet Tubman of the Bucktown District found freedom for herself and some three hundred other slaves whom she led north. In the Civil War she served the Union Army as a nurse, scout, and spy."

I look over at her and swear I see slight tears glistening in her eyes as she looks up at the sign bearing her accomplishments that she cannot read. I take her by the arm and we catch up with the rest of the crew.

"I didn't know you worked for the army," I say after a while.

"My sister was the first woman to ever plan and lead a military operation," Moses says. "They don't put that in the history books."

"How did you end up planning a mission for the U.S. Army?" More than anything I'm upset at my education because I didn't know any of this before today.

"I had a whole lot of jobs during the war. Half the time I was trying to find a way to raise money for my family and other Negroes that had made it up north. I used to run a little food shop during the war to feed the soldiers. That's how I ended up working for them. They used to love my cooking. I would make biscuits, gingerbread, and whatnot and sell it to the soldiers."

When I hear her talk about her life, I don't know when she ever would have had time for a break. When did she ever have time to just catch her breath?

"Was this the main way you made money?" I ask.

"There wasn't a lot of work for women, let alone a Black woman who couldn't read or write, in the North."

"Did you ever want to learn to read or write?" *When?* I think to myself almost immediately. *Between freeing seven hundred slaves, cooking for an entire army, and everything else she managed to accomplish?*

"Wasn't a matter of wanting," Harriet tells me.

I hang my head in shame and mutter an "of course."

"I can't read neither," Odessa says cheerily. "It never occurred to me that I should. But Buck and Moses can read. And of course Quakes. He's written any number of pamphlets."

"Mostly concerning the abolition of slavery and the rights of God's living creatures, great and small," Quakes says, puffing on a fat blunt I didn't see him light. "But former slaves, Black people who were born free, and poor whites rarely had the privilege of attending school. Working at a young age was very common."

I guess families were really "all hands on deck." It must have been very rare for a woman to be the breadwinner. Basically, everything about Harriet Tubman is a social anomaly.

"The soldiers loved when I came by," Harriet says, returning to her work as a cook for the army. I hope I haven't offended her about my reading comment. "I always came with something cheap and good to eat. Plus, I used to run the wash house down there. When you hand somebody clean clothes, they sure are happy to see you. I even started making friends with the folks in charge. That's when I run into Colonel James Montgomery. Rough-looking fella for how young he was. Time didn't do him no favors. He was another one with a big, unruly beard. Hair was looking all kinds of crazy. Every time I saw him he had on that blue jacket. You learn to feel a little bit of safety when you see a man in a blue jacket. You see one of them gray coats and your blood will run cold." It looks like a shiver runs down her spine.

I have to ask, "Did all the white abolitionists look unkempt?"

Quakes looks up at me and I try to avoid his gaze, though I can't help but notice the crumbs in his beard. That man sure loves his muffins.

Harriet snaps her head at me. "Now, all the white folks fighting for the North wasn't abolitionists. That's a common mistake. I'll give it to John Brown and the colonel, but not Abraham Lincoln. It would drive me mad to hear folks talking about Lincoln like he was the one that did all the fighting to free our people."

"Well, that's what they teach us in school," I say back to her. "They teach us that Lincoln was a great abolitionist." She stops walking, anchoring me in place with her, my arm still locked in hers.

"The hell he was, and I wish folks would stop saying that!" she counters. "That white man wasn't looking out for us. Do you know that he wanted all of us to move? I mean he wanted Black folks to leave the country. That was his bright idea to end slavery. He called a whole lot of upper-crust abolitionists to the White House and recommended that we all go to Liberia or Central America. So please stop telling everybody that Lincoln was some kind of abolitionist."

I feel reprimanded. Harriet unlocks our arms and storms up ahead toward the lone little church. I didn't realize this would upset her so much.

"I'm sorry," I say, trying to catch up to her. "I was just repeating what I had been told."

"And that's the problem," she tells me, still angry. "The wrong things are being handed down. Hell, at first I wasn't even sure the colonel was an abolitionist, but he for sure proved himself."

This is another time that I feel embarrassed that I don't know who someone is. I hate that so much of this country's history was not taught to me in school. But at some point, I guess I have to take responsibility for my own ignorance. My mother always instilled in me the importance of our history but somewhere along the way I stopped listening. I had a hard time accepting my Blackness because my Blackness had a hard time accepting me. My mother also instilled in me the fear of God, and I've spent my entire life learning not to be afraid.

Harriet then turned her ire to the appearance of the soldiers. "Lot of those young boys wanted to wear hair on they face because they thought it made them look older and more respected. I thought it made them look *messy*. Plus, most of them couldn't get they hands on a razor no how."

When Harriet talks about these historical figures it just seems like she is recounting stories from old friends. It never seems as grand as I make it out in my head. Maybe it's her incredible modesty. I mean the woman really doesn't have an egotistical bone in her body. It's this amazing juxtaposition between being raised to believe that you were lower than dirt and also knowing that you have done things that probably no other person could've done.

We reach the church and I'm suddenly gripped with fear. Everyone, save for Buck, streams in, but I hang back.

"You coming or you just gon' watch your shadow grow?" Harriet asks me.

"I just . . . need a minute," I tell her, and walk toward a cluster of trees.

I just keep thinking about the talk I had with Buck and Quakes about religion. I wonder if they had any words with Harriet about my thoughts on the subject, and if that would upset her. Let's just say I have a deep-rooted fear of letting down powerful women.

I'm starting to feel like I'm hiding something from her. I'm just trying to gather my thoughts so I can present them in a way that makes sense. Every time I have ever helped anyone with music or an album there is a back-and-forth, an exchange of ideas and history, but I'm so afraid for Harriet to learn about me that I just keep everything to myself.

"Darnell!" Buck has come looking for me. I didn't know he cared. "You okay, nigga?"

I rush out and touch him on the shoulder. He moves insanely fast for a man that big.

"Don't grab me like that, man!" He turns around with his fist balled up.

I don't think I need to explain that this is terrifying. His fist is the size of a Christmas ham.

"Sorry," I say quickly. "I just wanted to talk to you in private for a second."

He looks around at the wall of trees surrounding us. "It don't get no more private than this."

"Did you umm . . ." I look over my shoulder to see if anyone else might have followed Buck here. I blurt out, "Did you talk to Harriet about our religion chat? 'Cause I don't want her to think I am a heathen or anything." He just pauses and looks at me for a solid five seconds.

"I ain't out here telling nobody your business, but it sounds like there's something else you really don't want Harriet to know."

This completely throws me. It's not like I don't know what he's talking about, but I can't believe he's calling me out right here and now. "What do you mean?" I ask him.

"Man, you know what I'm talking about," he says, placing his hand on my shoulder, the weight of which feels like a satchel full of lead. "You ain't the first William Dorsey Swann I ever met, let's just put it that way." And he turns and walks back to the rest of the Freemans.

"Who?" I call after him, but he's disappeared through the trees. I'm sweating now. It's not profuse, but I imagine it looks concerning. My knees feel a little weak and I walk out of the woods to find Harriet standing there, waiting for me.

"Boy, what's wrong with you? You look sick," she says,

reaching up and putting the back of her tiny little hand on my forehead. "Oh chile, you wet as a horse's kiss. Come into the church and sit down."

I try to argue with her, because church is the last place I want to be, but I should know by now there's no arguing with Harriet Tubman.

The church has been abandoned for I don't know how long. It looks like no one's paid a visit, at least not in my lifetime. The roof is badly damaged from water rot and the pews are held together seemingly by faith and good fortune. Still, Harriet tells me to sit, so I sit. Odessa and the others start to gather around me out of concern but Harriet tells them not to crowd me and kicks them out of the church. Very unchristian-like behavior, if you ask me.

"Must've been something I ate," I tell her, buying time. "I just need a moment. Tell me more about Colonel . . . umm . . . John . . . what was it?"

"Colonel James Montgomery. He was the one that asked me to get involved after several of his men told him who I was. Said he overheard one of them calling me the General and wanted to know how a cook and laundrywoman had outranked him." She lets out a loud and strong laugh.

Her laugh kind of snaps me back to reality. I shake my head and clear my eyes. "That probably came as a shock to him," I say.

Harriet's laugh also invites everyone back into the church.

"Well, you have to realize that a lot of folks had heard of me, but I didn't make it my business going around telling people that it was really me. They had all heard of Black Moses or maybe Minty. They hadn't heard of Harriet Tubman. I had a new name and wasn't planning on going around bragging about what I been up to. Don't forget about the Fugitive Slave Act. Anybody that had once been a slave wasn't safe nowhere in the country. Let alone in a big town. Lot of folks thought I should've stayed up near New York so I could run into Canada if I needed to, but I had to go where I was needed the most. Plus, I still had to make money, after all. I done got most of my family escaped to freedom and I was the one bringing in most of the money." Harriet stops talking and just stares at me. "What you over there thinking about?"

I think the jig is up. I'm starting to really freak out. This place is starting to feel dangerous to me, and when I say "this place," I mean my own mind. I feel like I'm back in church on Sunday with my mother.

"Can you please uhhh . . . I just need a . . . excuse me for a moment?" My hands are clammy and I'm tripping over my words. I'm not as articulate as I normally am. I rush over to Buck and pull him into the corner. He is only moving because he wants to. I don't have the strength to actually move his body. I have to stand on my tiptoes to angrily whisper to him.

"If you told everyone here about me I'll . . . "

Buck crosses his arms in a very intimidating way. "You'll what?" he asks.

"I'll be hurt, Buck! I'll be really hurt. I've already gone through this once and I can't go through it again." I say this loud enough that everyone can hear me. And now they're all paying far too much attention to us.

"What the hell's going on over there?" Odessa asks.

"You know what?" My eyes are starting to tear up but still I stare Buck down. "There's nothing going on here. I gotta step away for a second."

I'm heading toward the door when I hear the hammer of a pistol cock behind me. It's a sound I have never heard in real life, but it was instantly recognizable.

"Don't even think about it," Harriet says. "I know somebody trying to turn back when I see it. You planning on leaving this room and not coming back. I know the look of somebody afraid to continue the journey. Now I done told you I'm in the business of getting people they freedom, and you ain't free, baby."

PART II

CHAPTER 8

I'M TRYING TO SLEEP OFF A hangover, but there is a
massive pounding on my front door. It sounds like the fucking cops are outside. This should come as a shock to literally
no one, but I don't like the police. They scare the shit out of
me. Here I am in my apartment scrambling to get my clothes
on and running around like I'm in trouble. As I stumble to
the bathroom to get my bearings, I notice there is a strange
body in my bed. "Strange" is one way to describe his body.
The other is "beautiful." He is one of those guys I know I
wouldn't have stood a chance with if I wasn't rich and famous,

and to be honest I'm not mad at that, because he couldn't have pulled me if he wasn't as good-looking as he is. I don't remember his name, but I can remember that we had fun.

As I hop on one foot to put my other leg in the pajama pants, I stop by the mirror and rub my eyes before opening the door. It's my manager, Suzzane. She is in her late twenties, but has the essence of a sixty-year-old mother with two kids in college and one that lives at home. She has her hair up in a very sensible bun, wears her glasses on the bridge of her nose, and dresses like a detective on a nighttime cop drama. I hate her shoes. She starts nosing around my apartment, cleaning up evidence from the night before, when she spots my . . . friend.

"He's gotta go!" she says, pointing at him.

"You can't barge in here telling me what I can and can't do in my own home," I say to her. "You don't have to go anywhere," I assure the half-awake and completely naked stranger in my bed. "What the hell is wrong with you?" I ask Suzzane.

She takes a step closer and talks out of the side of her mouth. "Dr. Slim is in a car headed over. He wants to pick up the pace on this deal." Then it quickly dawns on me what day it is.

"You need to get the fuck out of here!" I yell at him. I am now in full panic mode.

I frantically start to gather all of his clothes and begin shoving him toward the door.

"How am I supposed to get home? I live in Jersey," he says.

"Tell them at the front desk that Darnell will pay for your ride." I kind of feel bad because he had to get dressed in the hall. Suzzane is rummaging through my luggage to find an outfit for me.

"Why did you go out drinking last night if you knew you had a meeting in the morning? What sense does that make?" She grabs a pair of jeans, a sweater, and pair of Timbs and tosses them over to me one by one.

"You're the one who says I should go out and schmooze with the artists more. I'm trying to network," I say as I get dressed.

"Oh, is that what you and this little chocolate twink were doing last night? Were you networking? Did you make any lasting career connections? You think he has a connection over at NnSane Records, because the guy headed uptown right now is our main connection to other huge artists." I can tell she is biting her tongue. "And I can't believe you did this at an industry event of all places. What if someone had seen you leaving with Sisqó's stunt double? Then what?"

She is watching me struggle to put my socks on. "What if, Suzzane? What if someone saw me? Would it really be the end of the world? Would the walls of Jericho come tumbling down if someone found out I was gay?"

"Listen. I'm only doing what you asked. You asked if I could help keep this a secret and I agreed. I didn't ask to be mixed up in your shame." I stop dead in my tracks. I'm angry, but I know she is right.

"Okay, Suzzane! I'm not paying you to hurt my feelings. I'm paying you for professional advice." She picks up the boots and shoves them into my chest.

"You want professional advice? Butch it up, Mary."

Her phone rings and in one swift move she answers and is on her way downstairs to grab the good doctor.

Dr. Slim is one of the biggest names in hip-hop right now. Producing a song for him would catapult me into a completely new category. I keep my sexuality a secret because I know I'd be branded a "faggot" and no one would want to work with me. I *know* it. I mean, when Ellen DeGeneres came out it practically ruined her. And she's a white woman in comedy. What chance does my Black ass have?

I take a good look at myself in the mirror. I hate dressing like this. I feel like I'm doing a horrible cosplay of everyone that ever teased me in high school. I hate having to pretend like I'm something I'm not just to get ahead in my career. Before I can take a deep breath, the front door to my room flies open and Suzzane is standing there with Dr. Slim.

"Where da hoes at?" He is so much taller than I thought he would be. I'm almost a foot shorter than he is, and he is built like a daddy longlegs with dreads. His thighs are as skinny as my arms. He looks like he just stepped off the cover of *The Source*. I can't believe people dress this way in real life. The more I learn about the music business the less I can actually believe it. He has on a pair of Gucci pants with a white tall tee. And like three necklaces with huge pendants on them. They are all clustered together so they are hard to make out, but I'm pretty sure one of them is a Jesus piece and one of the others spells out "SLIM." His clothes are baggy, which exaggerates his skinny features. He moves in to shake my hand.

"Nice to meet you." I extend my hand and make forced eye contact with Suzzane as she clears her throat to remind me to code-switch. "Um, yeah, word to motha, lookin' forward to dis track, doe." I can't believe I'm talking like this. It feels offensive. If my mother saw this I wouldn't even be able to look her in the eye. Suzzane gives me a wink, and I hate it. It feels like I'm tap dancing.

"I like what you did on that Lil Genie track."

Suzzane, my hype man and personal devil, cranes her neck into our conversation. " 'Bad Bitch Boot Camp.' Number three on the charts, two times platinum, and the Grammy for Best Rap Song."

"Thank you, Suzzane," I say, both embarrassed and proud. Why couldn't I just be proud?

"I mean, a Grammy?" Dr. Slim says, staring me dead in my face. "That's what you fucking with? I'm trying to get on your level." He takes this opportunity to make himself very comfortable, grabbing a bottle of water from my minifridge.

"I'm not going to lie, I'm a little nervous about working with you," I admit. "Lil Genie was pretty small-time when we worked together. That track made her career take off, but I've never worked with someone as established as you." I don't know why I'm being so honest.

"Nah. You'll be good. I ain't worried about that," Slim says, putting his feet up on my couch. "We 'bout to make a hit. I just wanted to meet you face-to-face before the white boys start fighting. We got like three days, though. I hope Suzzane told you." He glances over at her and she is smiling from ear to ear. She looks ridiculous.

"You know, it . . . must have slipped her mind," I say as he heads back over to the minifridge. He takes another water for the road and pauses in the doorway.

"A'ight. Catch up soon." He slaps the doorframe and disappears. Suzzane and I both exhale at the same time and start screaming in celebration.

"Okay Darnell, please don't fuck this up. You think you can stay out of Chelsea for a week? I don't wanna see any paparazzi pics of you at Barracuda tipping a drag queen with an Absolut Raspberri and soda in your hand." I want to be offended, but she's really got my card. She even knows my drink.

"I'm not going to fuck up my career for a little fun. I have foresight." Eager to do a good job, I usher Suzzane out of my room so I can get to work. I strap on my headphones and immerse myself in Dr. Slim's discography, from his mixtapes in the early nineties when he went by Robbin' Dinero, to his brief stint in the rap group Banged Ur X, to his latest run of hits on NnSane Records. I have to understand his style and get a feel for the type of song he should make next. I need to know his story.

Rap's going through a transformation right now, we can do almost anything with it. Slim's got a really melodic flow that reminds me of some early eighties funk—the Whispers, the Gap Band—stuff we both probably grew up on. I pull a few of their records as well as some Euro dance stuff that's been worming through nearly every genre. It might be too poppy for Slim, but if he wants that Grammy, he's gotta play to the mainstream. By the end of the night, I've made a few beats from scratch with a rough chorus to pitch to him.

The next morning I wake up to an email from my lawyers telling me they are very pleased with his offer. Apparently, the man is richer than God and has no qualms about throwing money at his problems, which has worked out in my favor so I'm certainly not complaining. I am still nervous about working with him. I just get nervous around straight people in general. I wasn't in the closet before I joined the music industry at large, but now every time I interact professionally it feels like I have to hide a huge part of myself. It's not like I walk in the room and yell "I'm gay!," but I usually open my mouth and the jig is up. My voice always gives me away. I was always getting confused for my mother over the phone all through high school.

My entire morning routine is completely off. I bounce back and forth between listening to his music and freaking out about being surrounded by a bunch of straight men. I don't have time to get any food or anything so I'm feeling a little sick to my stomach. I've been recording myself doing my straight voice and playing it back to myself. Each time, I sound like a bully in an afterschool special made for middle schoolers.

I decide to practice a voice on the way to the studio. As I pass the clerk at the front desk I say, "Good morning to you, my man."

He literally takes one look at me and says, "Hey girl."

I'm crushed. "Can you literally tell that I'm gay just from how I walk by?"

"Yeah, girl. You're everything." While that is affirming,

it is also infuriating. I wish I had changed my outfit. What straight hip-hop producer wears a cape? At 10 a.m.? I double back and leave the cape with the clerk, fully aware I'll never see it again.

Part of me just wants to walk in and say "Fuck it!" I just want to be myself and work, but I'm actually not that bold. As I walk up from the train station, I'm already working on my posture, making sure not to stand so, ironically, straight. I calm my wrists from flailing. I try to remember not to purse my lips. I'm acutely aware of every inch of my body. Not just aware, self-conscious. I'm exhausted just walking, not swishing, over to the studio. When I finally get there, I realize that Slim has an entire crew with him. I don't know why I didn't expect this. There must be about five other people in the room. Most of them, I'm assuming, are straight. There's a guy that looks almost exactly like Dr. Slim. I mean he could be a stand-in. He probably is. Another, I'm assuming, is a bodyguard because he's built like a brick shithouse; he is dressed in all black and never speaks. Slim doesn't bother to introduce anyone. Clearly, I'm not going to go around the room asking, but in my mind everyone is straight until proven superior. I do not feel comfortable, but I put my best face on.

"What it do, man?" Slim says, extending his hand to me.

"Hey everybody, listen up. This is Darnell. This nigga out here winning people Grammys and shit, so we about to step our game up," he says, with one arm around me and the other gesturing about.

"I didn't win a Grammy alone," I say, embarrassed by my accomplishments. "There is a lot of work that goes into it. There's a whole team—"

He cuts me off. "Well, you 'bout to win me a Grammy. How about that? That's what I'm looking for." He gets right in my face, laughing with a huge grin. He's laughing so close to my face that I can smell the creamer he uses in his coffee. French vanilla. This is too much pressure. I feel like he might be kidding, but I'm not really sure. I'm not sure of anything around Slim. I've begun second-guessing every move I make.

"What you need to get started, my man?" Slim smacks the bodyguard on the back of the head, making him move so that I can sit in his seat. "You need some food, something to sip on? I don't know what y'all nerdy niggas be doing to get inspired. I know what I do. That's what Maxine is doing here," he says, referring to a bored-looking young woman somehow managing to roll a blunt with the most elaborate nails I've ever seen. Slim starts laughing and the room goes up. Maxine doesn't look up when her name is mentioned, she just lights the blunt, sits on a couch, and reads a trashy magazine. I wish I could be as unbothered as Maxine.

I sit down uncomfortably, feeling very small. I'm embarrassed for Maxine, but she really doesn't seem to mind at all.

"I don't need anything, thank you," I tell Slim. For some reason this response elicits even more laughter.

"I like you Poindexter niggas. Y'all funny as hell. You don't talk like no hip-hop producer. You sound like one of them white boys. Nigga, you sound like my lawyer." I'm not really sure how to respond to that so I just move on to the next idea.

"I actually started making the beats last night and even came up with a few melodies I think you would like. I was thinking maybe you team up with an R&B diva. It gives you cross-promotion, you would have access to a different fan base. That's how you cross over." I start pulling my laptop and hard drive out of my backpack. I made sure to carry a backpack instead of the bag I wanted to carry for fear of them calling it a purse. I mean . . . it basically is a purse.

I forgot to charge my laptop before coming here so I have to look for an outlet. Now I feel self-conscious because there isn't an outlet near the seat he cleared for me and I'm going to have to ask someone to move so that I can sit somewhere else. I'm putzing around the room like Woody Allen, awkwardly asking people to move so that I can sit down and check for outlets.

"Why you so nervous, man?" Slim asks me. I turn around with my laptop closed and pressed to my chest with the cord around my neck. He calls me out in front of everyone. Here I'm thinking I'm hiding it well and apparently, I'm not.

"I just wanna do a good job," I say, and before I can stop myself, I blurt out, "And if I'm being honest, you kind of remind me of people that used to bully me in school. I'm nervous around people that I want to impress and I really want to impress you. I want you to think that I'm cool enough, Black enough, and . . . " I kind of trail off, fishing for words. As expected, Slim's crew starts to laugh at me, but to my surprise, he tells them to "Shut the fuck up," and he takes me aside.

"Look man." He sounds almost like an older brother. "You ain't gotta prove nothing to me. I know you Black. I ain't here to qualify your Blackness. Just be yourself and let's make some music." I don't know if he is giving me the go-ahead to truly "be myself" or if this is a pep talk he is used to giving. But it does feel nice to hear. I finally find an outlet and sit down to get to work. I play him a couple of sample beats I've made and even feel comfortable enough to play him the sample vocals I recorded. I'm starting to see why everyone is there. I thought it was just a big posse of friends, but they all give input on his music. Some of them give really good advice. There are a few moments where it feels like a few too many cooks, but overall it is pretty easy to work with everyone.

A few hours pass and people start to leave one by one. I'm really proud of the work we are getting done in the studio. I don't normally write songs this fast, but this is a huge opportunity so I'm making it work.

"You sure you don't want nothing to drink?" Slim asks me. He has had a few drinks himself. I just keep hearing Suzzane's voice in my head telling me to be professional.

"No thanks," I say as I'm putting the final touches on the track. This song is a banger, if I do say so myself, and it looks like Slim thinks so too, the way he's bopping his head and shaking his bony hips. He takes another sip of his drink and walks the last person to the door. When he closes the door behind them, he just stands there without moving for about twenty seconds. It's a little awkward, but I just assume he's a little drunk. I'm starting to transfer the file over to a thumb drive so that I can get out of there and he mumbles, "I wanna thank you, Darnell. This track is really fucking good."

"Yeah, I think this is going to be received very well," I say. The file transfer is finishing up.

"I'm going to have another drink," he sort of mumbles, making his way back to the wet bar. "You gotta work with some more people, man. I'm about to make you famous as hell. They gon' eat you the fuck up." The more he drinks, the more he amps up the vulgar language. I don't want to take anything he says too seriously, though. You know people always make a lot of promises with a little booze in the system. If he keeps drinking, I'll be the new CEO of NnSane Records by the end of the night.

"I wanna be able to recommend you to people but we

gotta work on some stuff first. I can't be out there trying to vouch for your ass and not even know you like that. You ain't 'bout to embarrass me." He chuckles to himself. His jokes don't seem to hit as hard without his crew around.

"Here is your copy of the track. I will send the master to your manager, and I'll have a copy too." I extend my hand to give him the drive, but he doesn't take it. "You aren't planning on driving yourself home tonight are you?" I ask. He does not respond. He's just looking down at his drink. He's not even listening to me. Then without looking up he mutters "gay." Just one word.

I'm so scared that I don't know what to do.

"Excuse me?" I ask him. My hand holding the drive is shaking.

"Gay, nigga! Are you gay? Please don't lie to me." He's still looking at his drink.

"I don't want to cause any trouble or anything, I can leave now," I say as I slide my laptop into my backpack. It's so tense in the room. I am standing, but I move very slowly. I'm moving about like a person trying not to upset a wild buck in their front yard.

"Answer me, man. Are you gay or not?" He finally looks up at me. " 'Cause I am."

CHAPTER 9

SLIM STARTS CRYING. I HAVE NO idea what to do. I don't know if I should hug him or tell him that I'm gay, too. So I just stand there.

"That's okay," I say. Why the hell did I say that? Why would that be my choice? I grab his drink out of his hand and sit him down.

"Don't make me the only honest motherfucker in this room. I know you gay, too."

I just kind of trip over my words for the next few minutes while I rub his back. "I don't . . . I mean . . . Isn't sexuality a spectrum? . . . and . . . " It continues like this for way too long. "How did you know I was gay?" I finally ask.

"Come on, man! My grandma knows you gay and she

blind, deaf, and been dead for five years." Okay, that was a good one and I have to laugh.

"Then why did you let me put on that whole straight charade if you knew the whole time?" I feel like I could have been a lot more productive if I wasn't worried about trying to present myself as a straight guy all day.

"That was supposed to be you acting straight? Oh shit." He bursts into laughter. "Nigga, you don't know how to act straight. I been acting straight for ten years, and I feel like I can't tell nobody. I don't know why I'm trusting you. I feel like we in the same boat."

On the one hand I'm honored that he thinks he can trust me, and on the other hand, this feels like a lot more information than I bargained for.

"You haven't even told your friends from today?" I ask, referencing his entire crew.

"They ain't my friends. They on the payroll. That's my creative team, we got put together by the label." He seems really stressed out, which is fair. He's pacing and rubbing his hands through his locks.

"And you can't tell nobody!" He stops pacing and makes direct eye contact. "I'm not joking, man. I wanna be cool with you, but if you fuck up my money, we are going to have a real problem."

I don't like his tone at all. It's giving very DL vibes. "Hey,

I didn't ask you for any of this information. I didn't ask to work with you, and I for sure didn't ask you to tell me any of your secrets." There is an awkward standoff between us. "I'm not going to out you, Slim. I would never do that to someone, 'cause I know how much that scares me. So I promise you, I won't do that to you."

He finally exhales. "A'ight man. You good. Sorry, I'm tripping. I need to call a car. I drank too much. I'm wilding right now." He sits down in a chair.

"Let's go to the street and get you a cab," I say while grabbing my belongings.

On the way to the street he cries a little bit more and I struggle to get him in the cab. He even tries to take a bottle into the back seat. I have to yank the bottle out of his hands and throw it away. He is surprisingly strong for someone so skinny.

"Please take him to Thirty-Fourth and Sixth." I try to hand the driver money, but he refuses to take it.

"I don't take drunk passengers." He waves his hands in my direction. "If you want, you can get in with him or he has to go." The driver puts the car in park, so I think he means business.

I climb into the back seat. "All right, let's make two stops."

On the ride to his place, he falls asleep on me, but it doesn't feel inappropriate. He's resting his head on my shoulder and breathing very heavily with the smallest amount of drool about to drip onto my very expensive sweater that I wore to impress him. That cape really pulled the look together.

On top of being drunk, I think he is also exhausted. He seems like a child. Like a sleepy little kid tired after a long day at Six Flags. He is clutching his backpack in his arms, with his feet up against the back of the passenger seat. As I'm looking out the window with the city passing by, I feel calm. I don't feel scared, nervous, or ashamed in any way. This is the first time I've felt comfortable all day. I don't feel intimidated by Slim at all. He seems so vulnerable.

As we pull up to his building, I shake him to wake him up. "All right! We're here! Time to go!" I say while sliding him off my shoulder. He slowly starts to wake up. And I finally get a chance to make eye contact with him.

"Listen, man. Thanks for everything," he says, with tears in his eyes. "I got you." He grabs my shoulder and squeezes with as much strength as he can muster. "I want you to know I got you. If anybody ever tries to fuck with you, they are gonna have to deal with me. Okay?" He drags himself out of the cab, stumbles for a second as he gains his footing, and heads into his building. He doesn't even look back. I guess I was expecting one last wave or something.

My defense mechanisms will not allow me to believe that

he has my back in any way. Part of my brain is telling me, *There is no way someone in this business could understand me, let alone stand up for me if anything ever got weird*, but I'm allowing myself to feel good about the night. The cab pulls away and before I realize it, I fall asleep too. Now that I think of it, the night really was exhausting. Taking care of a drunk person is like babysitting, but in this case the child was bigger, stronger, and richer than me.

The later it gets into the night, the more I get nervous all over again. It's not like we were able to have a long conversation about discretion or anything. I'm just going to call Suzzane. It's so late that for some people, it's now early. I'm not even sure if she'll answer.

"What's going on? Is everything okay?" she asks. She sounds surprisingly awake for the hour.

"I'm fine," I say quickly. I'm trying to sound as together as her. It's not helping that I've started drinking by this point. "I had a really weird day . . . " I pause for dramatic effect. Maybe my aunt Hazel was right when she called me a drama queen at the age of nine. In her defense, I did respond to being grounded with Whoopi Goldberg's "I'm here!" monologue from *The Color Purple*.

"Darnell, what are you talking about? It's five a.m." It sounds like she is moving around the house. Suzzane has always been the type to work out in the mornings.

"Dr. Slim is gay!" I just blurt it out.

I immediately regret it. I hear her drop the phone and she is fumbling to pick it back up.

"What the fuck did you just say?!" She finally gets the phone up to her ear.

"I'm drunk. Please don't tell anyone! I swore I wouldn't tell anyone. I don't know why I even called you." It's too late now. I've let the cat out of the bag. This immediately makes me wonder how many people Suzzane has told about me. I wasn't able to hold Slim's secret for twelve hours, and here I expect Suzzane to take this to the tomb?

"Like, is he out to other people?" she asks.

"I don't know, Suzzane. I didn't do a full-on Diane Sawyer interview with him. He just broke down and told me. I'm begging you not to tell anyone. Please promise me you'll keep this to yourself." My voice is shaking and she can probably tell that I am scared. Good lord this day has been an emotional roller coaster.

"I promise." Now I can breathe.

"I need to go to bed. It's been a long day." We say our goodbyes and the next thing I know I'm waking up a few hours later.

My alarm is going off, I'm still in my clothes from last night, and I have a massive headache. I look over at my phone and I have five voicemails. That's never a good sign.

I pour myself a mug of hot water and make myself some tea with honey and down two ibuprofen so I can take the bad news.

"*Hey, Darnell. It's Slim.*" How did he even get my number? I guess when you have money you can get anything you want. "*Not sure how I got home last night, but I'm assuming you had something to do with it. I appreciate that. I don't know what I said last night, but I'ma need you to call me back and fill me in on the details 'cause my brain is fuzzy as a motherfucker. Call me back.*"

I choke down a huge gulp of lukewarm black tea. I was hoping he would just forget about the evening and we could continue as we were before. I click the next message. "*Hey man! Looking for a call from you. I know you're getting these messages. Call me back.*" The tone in this one has certainly shifted and it's clear that he is losing his patience. I need another cup of tea. No caffeine this time. I might as well finish the messages. "*Darnell. I'm headed over.*" I instantly hear a knock at the door. Fuck the caffeine, my heart is racing right now. It feels like he was waiting outside for that specific message.

"Good morning!" It's Suzzane. She's holding a breakfast sandwich in a greasy brown paper bag and a cup of fresh squeezed orange juice.

"Suzzane, you scared the shit out of me." I snatch the

bag out of her hand and make my way over to the kitchen table. "I thought you were Slim." I plan on finishing this sandwich in just two bites.

"Why would I be Slim?" Of course, her asking reminds me that Slim is indeed on his way over right now. I'm guessing that the other two voicemails were from Suzzane, telling me she was on the way over. Between brushing my teeth, changing my clothes, washing my face, and looking out the window every forty-five seconds to see if Slim is arriving, I manage to make myself somewhat presentable.

"Suzzane, I really need you to leave now. You can't be here when Slim arrives." I'm struggling to put in my contacts and not be nauseous, but tilting my head back and moving quickly isn't helping.

"I'm not leaving," she says as she finally takes her coat off and sits on the couch. It's very defiant. "I'm your manager and this feels like something I'll have to navigate managing down the line." I peek out the window and I can see a black Subaru pulling up to my building.

"He's here. Shit! All right, please don't be weird."

I quickly run to the bathroom to splash some more water on my face and pop a few Tums to ease my stomach pain. He knocks really softly.

"Hey, sorry I didn't return your calls," I say as I open the door. "I didn't get a lot of sleep last night."

He immediately starts to walk into the apartment. "It's cool, man. Oh shit. Hey, Suzzane. My bad. I didn't know you was having company." He shifts gears in tone.

"I didn't know I was having company either." I stare directly at Suzzane, who stares directly back at me. "In fact, you're both surprise guests this morning. I kinda feel like the most popular girl in school right now." Slim laughs.

"What brings you out, Slim?" Suzzane is still staring me down and slowly turns her attention to Slim, awaiting his answer. I don't know what she's up to, but I know I don't like it.

"Can we talk somewhere?" Slim asks. Jesus Christ, this whole situation is so uncomfortable. I would just like to be on the other side of it already.

"For sure, I just need to clean this up first." I walk over to the table and really take my time putting away the few dishes that I used to make my tea. I'm just trying to buy myself some time.

"Suzzanne, we'll be right back. We can finish up in a few." I lead Slim into my office.

Awkward. Uncomfortable. Uneasy. Stiff. I hate this. You know that thing you do when you can't make eye contact so you just start grabbing stuff. I'm exploring my office like I've never been in it before. Picking up pencils, looking at the ceiling.

"So what's up?" I manage to look in his direction, but not at his face.

"Darnell. I don't wanna be weird, man. I'm really grateful for what you did for me last night. You took care of me." I shift my eyes up.

"Of course. You looked like you needed help."

"I do need help. I wanna come out."

Did he just say what I think he said? I finally look Slim in the eyes. And we're just staring at each other, frozen in space, not a word between us. Talk about a pregnant pause.

"How would I help you with that? I'm not even out." I just don't see where I come in on this one. "I helped you get to your apartment because I didn't want to see you get hurt, or leave you in the studio overnight. I don't know if I can help you more than that."

"We can both come out together," Slim says. He looks like it took every bit of courage in his body to say this out loud. He is so exposed right now. "I been thinking about it and I think I got a good plan. See, I'm a big name in hip-hop. You got a good reputation. I feel like if we support each other, it would work. Especially if this song pops off. If this song is a hit there is *no way* anybody would be able to say shit to us." The fact that I'm actually even considering this is wild to me. He looks at me. "Do you wanna do it?"

"DO IT!" Suzzane yells from the other room. This scares

the shit out of me. She is really on a roll today. She barges in without knocking or anything. "This could be the biggest thing to happen all year, and if you release the song in May it could be everyone's Pride summer song." Leave it to Suzzane to immediately talk about monetizing my experience.

"Have you talked to your team about this yet?" I ask. His entire demeanor changes.

"I ain't talk to nobody but you." He points to Suzanne. "And I guess you too now."

I take a deep breath and can't really believe I'm about to say this: "If we come up with a good plan I'm down."

CHAPTER 10

"PLEASE STOP MESSING WITH YOUR HAIR," the hair-dresser tells me. I can't stop, though. It's a nervous twitch. This is a pretty big day for me.

"Sorry. I'm not normally this nervous. I'm more of a behind-the-scenes type. When I have to get in front of the camera, I just freak out." I'm still rubbing my hair and bit-ing my nails. Suzzane walks over to the swiveling chair and swings me around a little too fast.

"This lady doesn't want to hear your life story. You're going to tell that in front of the camera. She just wants you to leave your hair alone. Can you do that?" I am full-on sweating now.

"Don't patronize me, Suzzane. I don't wanna end up in a bad mood. Right now I'm teetering between feeling good about this and running the other way, and you're very close to pushing me in the wrong direction." I'm starting to think that Slim isn't going to show. That would be pretty shitty.

I keep thinking of worst-case scenarios. He hasn't given me any reason to believe he wouldn't make it. I guess I have trust issues. Suzzane makes room for herself right in front of me. She really has no qualms about taking up space. Maybe I should take a page out of her book. Without checking with me, she takes my bags off the table and tosses them on the couch. Normally I would call this behavior out, but I'm really trying to keep my shit together.

"Okay, I know we've gone over this a thousand times, but you can never be too sure . . . " Suzzane says, sitting on the edge of the long coffee table facing my chair with her feet on either side of mine. "Do you remember everything they said to you?" She looks over the rim of her glasses.

"Everything?! No! I don't remember everything. I remember the bullet points. Talk about how I didn't feel safe coming out. Talk about letting my art speak for itself. Talk about having a family, and—"

She cuts me off before I can even start to form the next words. "And remember to let Slim lead the conversation. He has to come out first. He is the name here. He is the reason we are going to get eyes on this segment." I feel like an accessory. I don't know why we couldn't just each come out on our own.

"When you say it like that I feel like an afterthought." She grabs both my hands in her own.

"I don't wanna say, 'Know your place,' but . . . know your place. You have to accept that we are riding on Slim's coattails here. He is in the driver's seat on this one. Trust me, this is the absolute best way to go about this."

I don't know why Slim isn't here yet. He's not exactly known for being on time, but I can't imagine he'd be late for live television. "I know we shouldn't bother him, but can we just call him and see where he is?" The hair lady has come back over to pick out my 'fro again.

"Hey!" Slim walks in the door. "Sorry I'm late. Traffic and shit." Of course he isn't alone. I feel like big celebrities are never really alone. There are always so many people following Slim around, asking if he needs anything, and bringing him water. That's another thing you learn when working with famous people. They drink a lot of water. His publicist, who has been coaching me on this entire fiasco as well, is typing in his BlackBerry and talking at the same time.

"Rip the Band-Aid off," he says to Slim, without looking up from his handheld computer. "You couldn't be in a better position. You're the perfect person to be doing it, too.

Well, you and . . ." He glances over at me as I'm brushing my palms against my pants to dry them. "Daryl?" I pause because I hear something that sounds like it's supposed to be my name.

"Darnell! My name is Darnell!" I extend my hand to shake his even though this is probably my fifth time meeting him. He does not shake my hand. I don't even think he saw it, to be honest. He seems preoccupied.

"Sorry, I'm bad with names." He shifts his focus back to Slim. "Just don't try and speak for the gay community. Speak from your own experience and you should be fine."

"Man, you doing too much. Chill, I know how to talk to people." Slim walks over and sits next to me, moving my bags from the couch back to the table. "Man, I'm glad you doing this. This shit got me nervous as hell. I don't really have that many friends in the game, but after this . . . I don't know." He seems really hesitant to say anything. He's oddly protective of the hip-hop community. I guess I can't blame him. I have a hard time in hip-hop, too.

The closest thing I've ever had to a mentor was the late, great Big House. But to me, he was simply Christian. Christian Hollingsworth, one of the whitest names I've ever heard on one of the Blackest dudes I've ever met. He was really big in the Miami scene in the early nineties, and he hired me as an "intern" when I was still in college down there. I don't know if most internships involved rolling blunts and, on at least one occasion, stashing a loaded gun, but I learned a lot from him. Through Christian, I got to produce my first track . . . geez, ten years ago, "She Be Leakin' " with the 305 Skwad. It's a filthy track, really misogynist and kinda terrible, but the beat was pretty good. And it put my name on the map. From then on, though, I tried to work with mostly women. Not only did writing about dick come easier, pun intended, but the women often had entourages with gays, so the experience was more comfortable for me on a personal level.

House was pure charisma. A great bear of a man, he was always dressed in Coogi sweaters, even in the Miami heat, like he was a Golden Girl or something. And he always had a posse of hot young boys that no one talked about. The Chocolate Twinkz he liked to call them. Christian was also gay and in the closet. As I said, I learned a lot from him. He was married, to the rapper H00d KunT, who was a big old lesbian. But it worked for them, I guess. They even had two kids. But they also had their own lives on the side. I later learned that Christian hired me because he knew I was gay, though I wasn't quite young or hot enough to be one of his Twinkz, thankfully.

House produced bangers and people just let him be. As long as he made hits, he would be okay, or so he thought. And when the hits stopped coming, he planned on retiring on a remote island somewhere with his Twinkz. He had two or three that were really special to him, but I think he only loved one of them, his Bottom Twink, this beautiful Jamaican boy named Raphael. If he loved Raphael, he never showed it. In public, anyway. Christian always said he would die before he came out. And sure enough, he did. He knew coming out would kill his career. I'm not so sure it won't do the same thing to Slim. Or me. I can't blame him for preferring to die than face the truth.

To deflect any suspicion, Christian would be the most homophobic, most transphobic, most misogynistic guy in the room. He had to be the hardest so no one would think he was soft. And according to House, he wasn't the only one in rap playing masc make-believe. There's a famous tale about how he pistol-whipped a guy in the parking lot of an Extra Supermarket because the guy rear-ended him, but from what Christian told me, there was a pistol being whipped but he was the one doing the rear-ending. I really miss his gay ass sometimes.

In the streets, House was respected, even feared, but in private he was the nicest, sweetest guy, and he took good care of those twinks. A couple of them were in his will. I don't want to say his double life killed him—the cancer didn't help—but I think death came as a sort of relief to him. But he loved the game more than anyone I've met. Hip-hop was more than music to him, it was the rhythm of our people, it was the soundtrack of our lives, it was our culture and it deserved our respect. His love for hip-hop deepened my love for it and I wouldn't be here without him. So, it's hard not to root for the people who crafted your life experience through music. No matter how problematic they may be.

"I'm sure your real friends will still be there after this is all said and done," I say to Slim, not quite believing myself.

He chugs his very expensive-looking bottle of alkaline water as if he were finishing off a pint of vodka and says, "I don't think I have any real friends."

Everyone in the room acts like they didn't even hear him say this, but I know they did. You would think they would all try to assure him that they are indeed his friends, but no one does. They just keep going on about their business.

"Hey man. We're doing this together. We're friends. You are not by yourself. I'm grateful to even have this opportunity. Not everyone gets a sensational coming out like this one." I'm trying to lift his spirits, but it really doesn't seem to be working.

Someone from production walks through the door holding a clipboard. "I would like to invite Slim and Darnell to set please."

That's it. This is my last moment to bail. The momentum in the room does not foster that feeling, though. It's as if we are all attached to each other. Everyone starts moving toward the set like a school of fish. Everyone instinctively turning and flowing together. Once we're in the hallway, the intensity is only heightened.

"Hey, I'm Smooth!" I hear a very familiar, distinguished, heavy voice with a lot of bass jogging up from behind us. I look over and Smooth has joined the school of fish, and is making his way to the front to lead us. "I'm the host."

Smooth is one of the most respected curators of hip-hop and R&B. He was a scholar of hip-hop before the music had even been accepted by the mainstream. If you haven't done a freestyle on his show, then you haven't made it. He has long gray dreadlocks and is wearing a black suit with a bright yellow head wrap. It's his signature look. The only facial hair he has is a military-style mustache with lots of gray in it. He has the stride of a high school principal. When he enters the room there is no question who is in charge.

"Dr. Slim, welcome back, my brother!" He walks right up to Slim. "When was the last time you were here? I ain't seen you in a minute. You must got some song you want me to promote." He lets out a deep belly laugh and grabs Slim by the shoulders.

"Yeah, I got a little something-something to share with everybody." They both sort of chuckle. "I do want you to meet somebody, though." Slim gestures to me. "This is . . . "

Like an eel jetting through water, Smooth glides over to me and grabs me by the shoulder. "I know Darnell Higgens. This man is the hitmaker. When I heard you two were going to be working together, I knew y'all were about to win a Grammy. This is a dream team. Do we get a little sneak peek today?" This is all happening so fast that I'm having a hard time keeping up.

"Well, you're going to get more than a sneak peek today," I say under my breath. In that moment, another producer swoops in and points us in a different direction.

"Sorry, Smooth, I have to steal them from you, but we'll take good care of them, I promise." She whips her clipboard around and starts scanning it with her eyes.

"All right, I'll see y'all on set."

I felt safer with him there. I'm definitely getting cold feet. I don't think I wanna do this anymore. The producer makes me snap out of it. "Slim, I know you've done a lot of television, so you know the drill. Please try and avoid looking into the camera and keep your eyes on Smooth. The live audience loves when you make eye contact with him. They can really feel the connection. In the first set we'll talk about the new song, then after the break we can catch up and we'll have time for fun . . . " Her voice kind of trails off and everything starts to blend together.

I feel lightheaded. I'm getting that feeling of blood

rushing to your head when you stand up too quickly. You can see everything happening around you, but your brain can't keep up and explain it all to you. It feels like I'm seeing the world in only shapes and colors, and I can only hear tones. Nothing is sharp. It feels like my head is underwater and I'm just moving around facing the sun with my head beneath the surface.

Suddenly, the sounds are all very sharp and reaching a crescendo. When I snap back to, I am sitting in a chair staring at Smooth and I'm on live TV. An audience of two hundred people are staring at the stage, staring at Dr. Slim in awe, staring at me in confusion. I don't know what I'm doing here either. Smooth is sitting behind a garish, faux solid gold desk with two fists holding microphones emblazoned with a seal facing the audience. Slim sits closest to him in a zebra-print chair and I'm on his right, sitting on leopard print. Smooth, much like hip-hop itself, isn't really known for subtlety. To the right of the stage, a DJ plays music to get the crowd hyped.

"Welcome back from the break, everybody. My first two guests are both stars in their own right. Darnell Higgins is a great producer who has done music for some of the biggest names in the hip-hop and R&B worlds. Now he's teaming up with Dr. Slim, who has more number one hits this year than any other artist, but he has been snubbed at the Grammys every year for the past five years. Well, this year they have teamed up and are trying to break that curse. Please welcome to our program, Dr. Slim and Darnell Higgens."

The audience starts cheering very loudly. I'm just blinking and looking around. I know the applause isn't for me at all, but I am going to soak up the noise anyway. The way Slim is so composed, it really is out of this world. He has changed so much from the defeated guy I just saw in the makeup room, to this completely confident man sitting next to me. His smile is so realistic. Even his skin looks better, maybe it's the stage lights.

"It's good to be back, Smooth." The audience lets out a little laugh. "You know if I'm gon' give anybody a sneak peek it's gon' be you." The audience cheers again. It seems like no matter what he says the crowd will cheer and applaud.

"So what's the song you two are working on?" Smooth asks, but he's looking at me this time. There is a long pause because I want to make sure he's expecting me to answer. I don't want to look stupid, but that ship might have already sailed.

"Oh sorry," I say, wiping my forehead. "I'm not used to being in front of the camera." The studio audience let's out an "aww" like I'm a cute puppy that just tilted its head in confusion.

"That's right, because you've worked in the studio with

some of the biggest names in R&B and hip-hop, yes?" This time I do not wait to answer.

"Yes, I have. It's kind of a word-of-mouth thing. One person talks about how great it was to work with you, then you're in business. Of course, three Grammy nominations don't hurt either." The audience really gets a kick out of this one. I'm getting more confident as we continue. The three of us are now volleying back and forth about the new song and our thoughts on the industry. Meanwhile, I am acutely aware of how flamboyant I get when I am relaxed or excited. Before I know it, it is time for a commercial break.

"You're a natural," Smooth says to me. I look over at Slim and his demeanor has changed again. He's back to the worn-down, insecure guy I saw in the makeup room before the show. He really knows how to turn it on for the cameras.

"Are you okay?" I ask Slim.

"I'm good, man. It's just a fucked-up day. This shit is too much." He's doing a lot of fidgeting. Someone brings over a couple of waters for the three of us. Smooth puts his hand on top of mine.

"You need to be in front of the camera more," he tells me. "You got a lot of charisma." This leaves me smiling from ear to ear.

"Thank you, Jack. That really means a lot coming from you."

Slim stands up. "I gotta use the bathroom." He doesn't even look at us when he says this. He just keeps his head down while some production assistant walks him to the bathroom. "I'll be right back," Slim says to Smooth and me.

Smooth says, "You better be back in less than two minutes. This is live TV."

Smooth turns back to me. "I feel like Slim is the first guy you've worked with. The ladies clearly love you." He is glancing over at me while they touch up his appearance with makeup sponges and a lint roller.

"They respect me because I respect them. I feel like a lot of producers in the industry are not particularly graceful when it comes to dealing with women in the workplace. So sometimes they would just rather work with someone they feel safe with." Smooth leans back in his chair and shoos his makeup team away.

"That's the kind of stuff we need to hear more about, my brother. Let's bring that up in the next segment."

Someone wearing a headset comes up to us. "We have forty-five seconds till we're on the air."

I'm looking around for Slim. I'm a little worried about him. He doesn't seem well. Smooth asks, "Where the hell is Slim?" Right as he asks, Slim joins the couch. He looks stressed out. Like he's been sweating. They start to count us down from ten.

He pulls me in and says, "I can't do this!" That's when the assistant director goes, "And we're live in three . . . two . . ." She points at us.

"What's good, everybody. Welcome back to *Smooth Live*, the number one hip-hop talk show in the world. I'm your host, Smooth, and once again, today I am joined by Darnell Higgens and the number one rapper in the country, Dr. Slim, to talk about their new song and a couple of other things. In fact, Darnell and I were talking during the break about women in hip-hop." He gestures to me so that I can fill in the studio audience. I'm still reeling from Slim's declaration right before we went live.

"Yeah . . . you were mentioning that I have a long track record of working with women in the studio. Actually, Slim is the first man I've worked with in hip-hop. I can't even believe you called me, Slim." Slim sits up in his chair and rubs his hands together.

"To be honest, man, that's why I wanted to work with you. I feel like you look at stuff different. You know."

Smooth looks over at him. "What do you mean?"

Slim looks me in the eyes, and I am starting to get very nervous. I don't like where this is going at all. He takes a deep breath. "I know that if I worked with a gay guy to produce a track, people might look at me funny, but this was my chance to prove that gay folks and straight folks can work together in hip-hop."

Everything that happens next is a big blur. This was not the plan at all. I hear people in the audience making a lot of noise, but I can't decipher if they are in support of me or not.

"I didn't even know you were gay," Smooth says to me.

"Well, to be honest, I didn't intend on telling you today." I'm scrambling to come up with some words and barely even know what I'm saying. "Normally, I'm very private about my love life, but I guess today . . . I'm coming forward." I feel completely powerless and deflated. We talk for a little while about why I decided to come out today, and about how we can bridge the divide between gays and straights in hip-hop, and the next thing I know we are off the air.

"What the fuck, Slim!" I yell at him. "Why the fuck would you do that on live television?" Smooth and his staff seem shocked by my outburst.

"I don't know, man. It just came out. I told you, I can't do this shit. I'm stressed the fuck out."

I circle around the desk and stand toe-to-toe with him. "You think *you're* stressed out. I just got outed on live TV! You told me you were going to do this with me, but instead you threw me to the sharks and kept the life jacket for yourself." Slim tries to get me to lower my voice, but I can feel the rug of my life being pulled right out from under me. "You made yourself the understanding hero, while I look like the outsider being thrown a bone by the benevolent king. Well, you're not a fucking king, Slim. You're a coward! And a queen just like me."

I storm out of the building without even grabbing my bags or waiting for Suzzane. I can't bear to see anyone's face right now.

PART III

CHAPTER 11

"DO YOU WANNA BE FREE?" HARRIET asks me with a pistol pointed at my face. Everyone in the room is afraid to move. Especially me. "I'm only gonna ask you one more time. Do you wanna be free? 'Cause we done come too far to turn back. In all my years of conducting, I ain't never lost a passenger and I don't intend to start today. Now, I'm gonna need you to get with the program." I have my hands up like she is a cop or something.

"Can you please put that away?" I ask her.

She slowly lowers the pistol. "Now, if you wanna talk about this we can," she says. "But if you make a move for that door it might be the last step you ever take. Don't you understand that you are taking this road for other people? It ain't got nothing to do with you."

I walk over to a pew and sit down. "Yeah, I know that." I understand that on a basic level, but when I try and apply it to my life, I have a harder time. "I was afraid for you to find out about me. When you're different you learn to hide a part of yourself away from other people for fear of rejection, or worse." I know deep down that this is a trauma response. Harriet walks over to me.

"When I help Black folks get to freedom, I don't ask them a bunch of questions about who they love and what they do. I only concern myself with where they need to go. You understand me? The biggest struggle in earning your freedom is feeling like you deserve it. Sometimes we feel like we ain't worth putting in the work." Her tiny little frame hovers over me as I kneel in submission.

"I didn't ask to be psychoanalyzed today. I just want to help you finish your album," I say, standing up, reminding myself that I am indeed much larger than she is.

"When you do this kind of work you have to look at yourself," Odessa says, stepping forward. "The road to freedom is long and you have a lot of time to think, about yourself."

"Listen. I really appreciate everyone helping me with my breakdown, but it's starting to feel like an afterschool special. It's a little heavy-handed. I understand that I have been very dramatic, but I don't want everyone coming forward one by one reading me their letters like this is an intervention."

Quakes is the only one making eye contact with me at this point.

"I'm gay!!! Sometimes I queen out. Get over it."

Harriet doubles over a pew with laughter. "Wait, that's your big secret? Baby, I think it might have been easier for me to hide twelve runaways in broad daylight than for you to hide that you're gay. We been knew that. Since the moment I saw you. Ain't nobody worried about that."

This feels like coming out to my mom all over again. I know I'm not the most butch, but people could at least act shocked when I tell them.

I look over at Moses. "Did you know?"

He just looks at the floor. I dart my eyes to Odessa. "How about you?"

She just chuckles and says, "My grandmother knows and she blind and deaf."

And right on cue, everyone chimes in, "And she's been dead for one hundred forty years!" This sends Buck into one of his laughing fits that I have grown numb to. He's one of those people that laughs and physically assaults you at the same time. I try not to stand next to him and say anything funny. I just end up covered in bruises. It does feel a little better to get this off my chest, but I can't help but feel silly for my emotions in the first place. I decide to take a step outside for a breather.

"Fine!" I yell like some spoiled child. "Y'all just laugh your goddamn heads off." As Harriet and Odessa quickly make the sign of the cross over their chests, I storm out of the church.

I'm just continuing with the dramatics. My mom used to say, "You must think you are the main character in a musical." I pace back and forth outside the dilapidated church before gently collapsing against its side, the back of my hand against my forehead, thinking, "If someone saw this right now they would be so moved." I don't have to wait long because here comes Moses.

"I noticed you stormed out," he says, as if I didn't just cause an entire scene.

I let out a slight laugh. "What gave it away?"

We just stare at each other for a moment.

"I know I'm not that different from all of you. I just tend to separate myself, to protect myself. I don't exactly see reflections of myself in history."

This seems to perk him up. "Darnell, that's on purpose. That is by design. And I don't mean in a conspiracy theory or 'the white man is trying to keep you down' sorta way. I mean queer people weren't allowed to be theyselves back then." He pauses for a moment to let this sink in. I stare at him and he meets my gaze before going on. "And the ones who did usually paid the price. And it sure wasn't cheap."

It never even occurred to me that queer people even existed back then, but when you stop to think about it, of course they did. It's not like being queer is a phenomenon of the new millennium.

Moses invites me to walk with him and I'm far too worn out and intrigued to fight him. "One of the fiercest Black activists I ever met was about as queer as a four-legged duck," he begins. "The Queen used to host these crazy dance parties, balls, in D.C. Now, I didn't make it to D.C. very often, but everybody knew about those balls, and I do mean *everybody*. The president even knew who he was." He pulls out some weed and rolling paper. "Hell, being Black in public was bad enough, let alone being Black and gay. He called hisself the Queen of Drag and everybody else just started calling him that too. Even the newspapers called him 'the Queen.'"

I wish I could've been a fly on the wall or a man in a dress at one of those parties. I inch closer to Moses as we walk. "Did he get caught?"

"He got caught basically every time he set up shop." Moses exhales elegantly and passes me the joint. "Somebody must've been telling the cops. When everybody know you, you don't get to keep secrets, 'cause everybody that know you . . . know somebody else. The cops used to throw him in jail—one time they kept him for three hundred days."

"Was he a former slave?"

"He sure was."

How did he do it? I wonder. How did this queer, Black ex-slave—in the late 1800s, no less—find a group of other Black folks that wanted to dress up in gender-bending clothes and have fun? I've been searching all these years . . .

"Did people actually come to the balls?"

"Oh yeah, they came all right," he says, the smoke encircling him like a halo. "There were so many people packed up in them rooms when the cops came, folks was jumping out of windows to get away." I'm finding myself picturing wigs and dresses and people flying through the air. "Everybody ran except the Queen. He would get right up in the officer's face and yell 'You is *no* gentleman!' Took a lot of nerve."

I glance at him and almost instinctively say, "It do take nerve," referencing *Paris Is Burning*, even though I know he doesn't get the quote. It's not for him. It's for me.

"He called hisself a queen because he was a leader in his own community. Lot of folks looked up to him because of how brave he was. He could read, write, organize, and most of all, he could attract. That's how he found his people."

Most of all, he could attract. Have I been pushing my people away?

"If you came to one of his balls and won a cakewalk, your status in the community would go up. You became something of a Black socialite. It really is amazing what somebody can accomplish when they have support. His name was William Dorsey Swann." Buck's words suddenly make sense. "Even his brothers used to help him throw these parties. William was about as out as a person could be at that time. I think you got some Swann in you too." *You ain't the first William Dorsey Swann I ever met.*

But I am certainly not leading any revolutions, or putting myself in danger so that people can express themselves. "No. Not me. I'm more of a behind-the-scenes type. I don't really like a lot of attention." I'm aware of how silly that sounds after running out of a church crying less than twenty minutes ago. What can I say? I'm a complicated woman.

"Now hold on!" he says with his joint dangling from his lips. "Not every leader is out on the front line with their face being posted for the world to see. For every Harriet Tubman, Frederick Douglass, and Sojourner Truth, there was a dozen abolitionists and activists working behind the scenes, risking it all to help us meet our true potential. Everybody wasn't made to be out front."

I like to think of myself as a critical thinker, as someone who looks at things from all perspectives, but for some rea-son it never occurred to me to consider all the people whose names will never be in our history books. I hadn't thought of the people whose names weren't even known in their time because of how risky it was to exist as an activist back then.

I imagine you can really start to have some survivor's guilt if you let yourself go down that rabbit hole.

"There is so much pressure to be great when you think about what has been sacrificed so that I can be free in this country," I say after a while. "All the people who literally gave their lives so that I can live 'loud and proud.' People sacrificing it all for me before I even existed. I guess that's why I'm so hard on myself."

Moses takes a long drag, smoking the joint till it practically disappears into his mouth, and says, "Just live, Darnell. Take it from there. Just live your life. Your freedom ain't contingent on nothing. It is yours. You know what Dorian Corey said. 'You've made a mark on the world if you just get through it. You don't have to bend the whole world. If you shoot an arrow and it goes real high . . . ' " Then we both say, " 'Hooray for you.' "

I guess he has seen *Paris Is Burning*. Or maybe queens have just been saying that for a hundred and fifty years.

CHAPTER 12

NOW THAT I HAVE COMPLETELY QUEENED out and caused a scene, the ride back to New York is a bit awkward. I assume that they aren't judging me, but I can't help judging myself. This is something of a pattern in my life. I get overwhelmed, and instead of openly and honestly communicating with everyone around me, I pretend like I'm not in distress until I can't pretend anymore, my pot boils over, and I just yell at all the people around me, or I cry like a child and just hope that everyone will forgive me. This group seems very forgiving.

"I'm sorry, everyone," I say, gripping the steering wheel too tight.

"Chile, ain't nobody worrying about that. We got too much to do to be focusing on you and your little temper tantrums." That hurts but it's also true. "You is allowed to be mad, you is even allowed to wallow in it for a little while, but you ain't allowed to stop moving. Not when we got places to go. Too many folk relying on you to make it." I don't have a response. I just look over at her like a sad little puppy. "You must feel so much better now that you got your little 'secret' off your chest."

I must admit it does feel better. I actually felt guilty keeping that part of myself from them. They are all being so open about such intimate details. If they are trusting me with such deep trauma, then I should be able to trust them with mine. Now it feels like we actually know each other, instead of me just knowing them.

At Harriet's suggestion, I take a few days off, just for myself. Without actually saying it, I think she wants me to practice self-care. I relax for a total of forty-five minutes before I grow restless. Instead, I get to work on the album. I didn't realize it at the time, but being at Brodess Farm was far more emotional for me than it was for Harriet. I could feel the history of the place pulling me down, but Harriet seemed almost relieved to be back. Maybe because she came of her own accord. And was free to leave just as easily.

Then there's that tale of crazy old John Brown, a white man who risked everything for what he believed in, eventually giving his life. And William Dorsey Swann! That just blew my head clear off my shoulders. How did a man like that survive let alone thrive at a time when he was barely considered a person? The last few days just are running nonstop through my head and it's all I can do to try to get it all down.

I spend my little hiatus almost completely working, making beats, writing songs. I feel like I'm being guided by some force greater than me, maybe it's God or maybe it's Harriet, or maybe it's a combination of both, but I haven't felt this inspired, this alive since . . . since Slim.

Late one night, over Chinese food, my curiosity gets the best of me. I haven't seen or talked to Dr. Slim in over ten years. Maybe more. I try not to think about him, but sometimes he creeps in. Or I hear a song of his on the block or see some post on social media about him. It's hard to avoid someone who can be anywhere at any time. I haven't heard much about him recently, but a quick search catches me up real fast. He's the head of NnSane Records. And he's . . . married . . . Is that . . . ? It's Raphael, Big House's Bottom Twink. That Twink really has a niche. Though I guess he's not a twink anymore. Their wedding photos were in *People*. I guess he came out after all. And everything worked out. For him. And here's a photo of Slim with Harriet, looking a mixture of pissed, terrified, and tired. But that's kind of how she always looks.

Slim signed Harriet and the Freemans. Was he the one

who got me involved in this project in the first place? I don't
know how I feel about that. On the one hand, fuck him. But
on the other, this project with Harriet is the best thing that
ever happened to me.

The next morning, I head back into the studio ready to
work and eager to show the others what I've been working
on. When I walk in, they're all standing around in a semi-
circle. I think they must be listening to Harriet but she's off
in a corner, chugging her boiling-hot coffee.

"Yo, D, my nigga." It's him. Dr. Slim. He's lost the dreads
and is wearing a very expensive-looking suit, but it's him, all
right. "Been too long fam, how you holdin' up?"

I used to fantasize about this moment, what I would say,
how Slim would react. I had rehearsed an entire speech and
revised it over the years. I would look him straight in the eye
and tell him how he had ruined my life. How nobody would
hire me so I had to resort to making commercial jingles. *I
had to rely on kitty litter to keep me afloat all these years because of
you*, I'd tell him. I'd really let him have it.

"Yeah. You too," I say sheepishly, and begin unpacking
my stuff.

"Don't know if ya heard, but . . ."

"You're the new head of NnSane Records. Yeah. I just
figured that out last night, as a matter of fact. Along with a
couple other things about you."

Odessa, Moses, and Buck rush to their seats while Quakes pulls up a little stool. They're all ready for the show. Only Harriet doesn't move, or show any interest in the drama unfolding in front of her.

"Listen, you wanna go somewhere and talk?" Slim looks at me from behind dark sunglasses. I'm excited because I finally get to say something I've only dreamed of saying my entire life.

"Anything you want to say to me, you can say in front of them," I tell him defiantly. I hear Odessa let out a tiny "Yes!" before clasping her hand over her mouth. "They've been nothing but honest and open with me. They deserve the same from me."

Slim looks around as Buck and the others lean in out of curiosity and just plain nosiness. "Maybe some other time," he says, adjusting the lapel of his Prada suit. At least his taste got better. He's about to leave when I stop him.

"Wait. I want you to hear something."

• • •

"Keep up the good work, y'all," Slim says a half hour later on his way out of the studio. He loves what he heard, or at least that's what he says. Our history doesn't make me want to trust him any more than I can throw his bony ass.

"I don't like that nigga," Buck says with Slim barely out the door.

"Me neither. Not after what he did to poor Darnell," Odessa adds.

While I'm touched by this show of solidarity, I'm also shocked and horrified. "How do you know about what he did to me?"

In unison, Quakes, Odessa, Moses, and Buck say, "You-Tube."

"Y'all sure do learn fast." To my surprise, I'm not mad or embarrassed. If anything, I'm kinda charmed by this new, incredibly invasive family. "Did it have like a million views?"

"More like sixteen thousand," Odessa says, like the annoying little sister she's become. Sixteen thousand? I don't know if I'm relieved or disappointed.

"If you're done lollygagging around," Harriet says, still in her corner, still with her steaming coffee, "we have an album to finish. And lest we forget, a show to produce."

I really want to get back to work, so I go right over to Harriet. "I loved what you said the other day about not stopping. Even though I was supposed to be resting—"

She jumps in, "And you shoulda rested. We all need to rest sometimes. It's important for the soul. Resting ain't stopping. You rest so you can keep going. I rest without even meaning to because tha Lawd wills it. But when it comes to getting free—you *stop*, you *die*. You stop and the people around you could die, too. No matter what happens you keep *going*. So let's get to work."

Everybody grabs their instrument and awaits my word, like I'm suddenly the Conductor. Without thinking or anxiety or hesitation, I take my place at the center of the room and direct Harriet to the mic. "Quakes, gimme a beat."

We're becoming a well-oiled machine. Once Quakes whips something up, Moses and Buck seamlessly join in, with Odessa providing background vocals. We're jamming in search of a groove. I nod to Harriet. "Can you tell me the feeling you get when you are trying not to stop?"

Harriet eases to the microphone and speaks passion-ately over the music. "I can tell you this. When you walking through the marshes and swamps, to avoid leaving a scent in the ten-degree weather, wearing only the clothes you left with, you don't need a lot of motivation. When you sleep for two hours after three straight days of nonstop walking in the dead of winter, you don't need a lot of motivation. It's really not that hard to motivate yourself to keep going when you don't have another option. After a while, you start to feel like it's normal to feel the way you do. You forget that we wasn't made to be slaves. You forget that you are a child of God. Truly a divine creation. When I think about how much I deserve my freedom, that's all the motivation I need." She doesn't say this with any amount of ego. The opposite, really.

"But what about other people?" I ask her. "What could possibly motivate you to risk it all for other people. I mean, you made it to freedom. Several times."

She snaps her head to me. "Don't you deserve freedom? How I'm supposed to live with myself knowing I could have helped somebody but chose not to? I can't enjoy no freedom like that."

She truly is an empath. She feels so deeply for others. Makes me question all the times in my life when I could've done more than I did . . . or could have done anything at all, for that matter.

"Okay, last question," I say. "What about motivating others? What do you say when they wanna turn around?"

"Well, first of all, I think you know the main reason I carry a pistol on me. It ain't in case we get caught, 'cause I ain't never been seen on even one trip. I keep it on me to let other folks know how serious I am about them moving forward, and I ain't about scaring nobody either. It's to let them know I mean business. When they see how serious I am, they get in line real quick. That's what it means to be a leader, Darnell." She looks squarely at me when she says this. "I got to lead people way bigger and stronger than me."

Harriet goes into a story about conducting passengers to Canada and one of them looked like he wasn't going to make it. This was after the passage of the Fugitive Slave

Act, meaning all Northern states had to return any captured escaped slaves to their Southern prisons. Harriet and her passengers had to get as north as possible, when Gettysburg used to be far enough. And this man felt some kind of way about it. They were just two days out from the border-state slave catchers.

"I think he was in his own head because he kept talking about how he would already be there if they hadn't passed the Fugitive Slave Act," Harriet continues. "Then he started to go down a wild path: 'If only the South hadn't relied on crops, if only Abraham Lincoln was a real abolitionist.' Eventually he got to a point where he said, 'If I wasn't Black I wouldn't have to deal with any of this.' I done heard enough out of that man."

Suddenly Harriet grabs the mic off its stand. "Well, you is Black!" The band picks up the tempo, matching Harriet's energy and aggression. "You is black as the toughest part of my shoe leather, and you gon' have to learn to deal with that! You can't talk to me about wishing you wasn't in this situation 'cause it ain't gon' help not one of us either. What about your children? Do you want them to go through this, too? Do you want them to feel like being property is normal, because you couldn't finish up two more days of walking? You got a chance to have free babies, so they can have free babies. Everything we do in this world ain't for ourselves. Some of it is bigger than us. This one of them things." She looks up at me. "When you Black, it's all for the next generations to come. It ain't never for us, remember that." Harriet drops the mic and walks off the stage.

These words really stick with me. It's one of those things you are always told, but one day it sinks in. I feel it even more so being queer. I don't wanna be anybody's role model, though. Sometimes I get so annoyed at the guilt and duty that comes with being a Black person in America. It's never enough to just do your own thing. It always has to be for the people who haven't come yet. Then again, I realize how much I have benefited from people going through what they went through.

"You paying attention?" Harriet walks up to me quickly and quietly, startling me. I didn't even realize she was still talking.

"Yes, ma'am. I'm listening." That is a lie. I look down at my paper and I write, "Whatever You Do, Keep Going." This feels like the perfect hype song.

CHAPTER 13

AFTER A FEW MORE HOURS OF jamming and refining, we lay down the tracks for "Whatever You Do, Keep Going." I don't mean to blow my horn, but call me "Taps" because this shit is fire. As we finish the song I am truly amped up to keep going. I am so motivated and excited that I don't realize that I'm almost salivating. Harriet looks at me and says, "Mmmm, I like that one. Y'all sounded so good." This compliment sets my skin aglow. I must be beaming from ear to ear. It means a lot to have Harriet say such nice things to me. I seek her validation more than I am willing or happy to admit. I think that love and acceptance from her feels like love from all the older Black people in my life who rejected me before.

My mother never rejected me, but she's never truly

accepted me either. She keeps hoping that being gay is something I'll eventually grow out of. I always tell her I'm a middle-aged Black man and God knows how prone we are to change.

"Thank you," I tell Harriet in an attempt to keep it simple. "I was worried you might not like some of the work I'm coming up with. I'm actually shocked that you even want to work on something like this." She raises her wispy eyebrows and scrunches her nose in my direction.

"What you say that for?"

I get a little embarrassed to admit my thought process.

"Over the years I thought I read somewhere that you didn't want to see any stories about slavery onstage and that—"

She cuts me off. "I know what you talking about. 'I've seen the real thing, and I don't want to see it on no stage or in no theater.' That the one you talking about?"

I kind of lose the excitement that I had before. "Yeah, that's the one. I've been thinking about that this whole time. I just remember you saying you didn't want to see any depictions of slavery onstage."

She takes a deep breath. "Chile, I ain't never say that. People make up stuff I said all the time. I sat there and told that woman my life story."

"Which woman?"

"That Sarah Bradford woman. She wrote my life story. Or a version of it, anyway. I told her everything I could remember, and she wrote down whatever the hell she wanted to. The way she had me talking in that book you would've thought I was Frederick Douglass. First time I heard somebody read it back to me, I was thinking, 'Hell, I don't talk like that. Who is this book about 'cause it sho' ain't me. That don't sound nothing like me.' Sometimes she took what I said and put it in her own words, and sometimes she just created what she wanted to write. I had the lady write the book 'cause I needed money for my family and this seemed like a good way to make some. Helped out a little bit, but not enough. Made it a little strange to go on the road and tell my stories again, though."

I think I finally get it now, why she's doing this. "Is this album your way of telling your story in your own words?"

"For this generation. And all the future ones. Today, you can say something and the entire world can hear it in seconds. I used to go out to these abolitionist-type meetings to tell my story for money. They had them in churches, tents, in the woods, ballrooms. They happened everywhere except the South. Before the war, these meetings used to send money to folk like John Brown and Frederick Douglass to help fund they abolitionist actions. Sometimes I would go and make some money to live off of. I helped other folks too. They would cart me out when they really needed to make those white folks with money feel guilty and open up they wallets."

"That sounds terrible," I say, knowing how naive I sound.

Harriet chuckles slightly. "If you think that's bad, sometimes they took some escaped men and asked them to show the lashings on they back to the supporters so they could see the reality and horrors of what we went through."

"Oh God . . ."

"But the lashings and whippings don't even start to touch on how we as a people been affected by slavery. Our goal was to get as many folks as we could to be abolitionists. We knew if we was gonna end slavery, we would need as much support as possible, and I understood what that meant for me. I was gon' have to make money using my experience, and ain't nothing wrong with that. You use what you got to get what you need, and baby, I got pain."

Damn. That's a great title, too. I jot down "Baby I Got Pain" as Odessa saunters over.

"Not all of us felt that way," she says. "People often tell stories about the slave experience as if we all thought the same. There were people who didn't want to relive their experiences by hearing about it in a book or seeing it onstage. For some of us it hurt too much."

Her eyes tell me she is talking about herself. "Is that how you feel, Odessa?" I try to offer some compassion.

"I used to. When I first got free I didn't want anything to do with slavery. I even tried to pass as a white woman for a while. Being light-skinned gave you a lot of privileges that my dark-skin family didn't have." She seems to carry a lot of guilt about this.

"Just like Ellen Craft. That woman sure know she was smart!" Harriet chimes in.

"Who is Ellen Craft?" I ask.

Odessa answers. "When you went to an abolitionist meeting there were three stories you really wanted to hear: Harriett Tubman, Henry Box Brown, or the Crafts. Ellen Craft and her husband escaped by train. Right in plain sight. They spoke to the white folks face-to-face. Lord, I can't even imagine."

I am so confused.

"Most of us was avoiding white folks altogether," Harriet adds, "but these two was sitting right next to them the whole way to freedom."

I finally ask, "How did they do it?"

Odessa takes over. "See, Ellen was light-skinned. She what they call high yellow. Her and her husband was able to purchase a train ticket with the money they saved up from him working as a carpenter and a cabinetmaker. They used the money to buy costumes and came up with a whole plan." Odessa starts to get very animated. "I actually got to meet

her once at an abolitionist rally with Minty. I had to go tell
her how brilliant she was. They hardly ever let women speak
in public spaces, except for Minty. Nobody would dare tell
Minty she couldn't speak." The group lets out a chuckle and
Harriet responds with a half-hearted flick of the wrist.

"I actually got to hear her talking in Newburyport, Massachusetts. There was almost a thousand people there. She
was so beautiful and elegant. Spoke like she knew how to
read and write. When she got up there she talked about how
they not only disguised her as white but she dressed up like a
white man! Can't even imagine the mindset she had to get in
to do this. William, her husband, played as her slave and she
played as a white slave owner. She didn't have a deep voice so
she pretended to be sick so she wouldn't have to talk, and she
couldn't write so she put her arm in a sling so she wouldn't
have to write anything! They thought of everything."

Odessa's excitement is infectious. She's got a real pres-
ence about her. We should give her a solo, I think, and make
a note and write down "The Ballad of Ellen Craft" next to it.

"One night they even had dinner with the steamboat
captain," Odessa continues. "Well, they took a train from
Macon to Savannah, then sailed from Savannah to Philadelphia and gained they freedom. Later on, they decided
to move to England to avoid the Fugitive Slave Act. We all
had to make a decision when that happened." Odessa stares

at me as if she is expecting more of a reaction. She has the excitement of a child giving a presentation on their favorite superhero.

I return her smile and excitement. "That's incredible."

Harriet walks over to me. "That what I mean when I say you got to use what you got to get what you want. This woman had light skin, a desire for freedom, and a whole lot of smarts." Harriet shifts her weight. "So you need to ask yourself: What do you got, and what do you want?"

CHAPTER 14

THE NEXT FEW DAYS ARE A whirlwind. I'm torn in five different directions at all times. One minute I'm perfecting a track with Quakes, the next I'm helping Buck with a particular riff, then Moses has an idea for a new chorus, and Odessa insists on scatting on every song, all the while Harriet is telling me a story about how John Brown and his sons massacred five pro-slavery men in front of their families in the middle of the night. I've never felt so alive.

We're averaging a song every few days. The whole band is scary talented, but Harriet's skills as an emcee have really impressed me. That two-hundred-something-year-old woman can spit. And her energy is next level. She can work into all hours of the night, except when she passes out unexpectedly on the microphone while recording. Which has happened more than once. She can be spitting the hardest rhymes you've heard and then all of a sudden she falls silent. I look up and she's drooling on her music stand.

I've started plotting out the show to promote the album, too. It's a lot. Producing music comes naturally, but putting a show together? That's outside my wheelhouse, but Harriet was very specific that she wanted me to do it. So I'm doing it. At this point, I'm thinking we just do a simple concert, no frills. Harriet Tubman should be enough for people. But even the logistics of putting that together involves so much work. It's taking a toll on me. I'm both tired and excited all the time. I'm not getting enough sleep. Instead, I wake up in the middle of the night and jot down some idea that come to me, and I'm too wired after that to go back to sleep, so I work some more on the album. My creativity feels like a faucet I can't turn off and then one day . . . I'm dry.

I'm starting to experience writer's block. I think I burned myself out. I was having such a good time, I didn't realize I was spreading myself too thin. Now I can't even make a single decision to save my life. Someone asks me a simple question and I give a complicated response that doesn't even answer the question in the first place. What's worse, we're nearly done with the album. We're so close. It's almost over.

And then there's Slim. I haven't seen him for fifteen years and now I can't get rid of him. All hours of the day and night. He keeps on "checking in" on our progress with video calls, texts, and emails. He's the president of a whole-ass company, you'd think he'd have more important things to do, or at least *other* things, but a lot is riding on this album. Or so he tells me. Over and over again. After he outed me, Slim used to dodge my calls and now he's suffocating me. He used to visit the studio every day but then Harriet banned him. He tried to argue but he learned what I and everyone else who tangles with Harriet Tubman learned: You're not going to win. So instead he's blowing up my phone.

The world, understandably, is interested in hearing what Harriet Tubman has to say. Slim and NnSane Records have been promoting the album like crazy, even though it isn't finished yet. I'm suddenly getting all these interview requests. I don't even have an agent. Suzzane left me years ago and started her own agency. I'm sure she's overthrown a small island nation by this point. I was only using social media for porn and overnight I have thousands of followers I didn't ask for. I left hip-hop before social media was even a thing and it's a mind trip to be thrown into the middle of it all.

This is too much pressure. If I don't finish this album on time . . . Screw Slim, but it feels like I'm letting down my entire race. This is by far the most important project I have ever worked on and I think I'm letting it get to me. I don't want the others to see that, though. I'm just looking at my laptop's blank page, writing and erasing the same two lyrics. It feels like everyone is just waiting for me.

"Do you have anything for us today?" Quakes says as he hops onto a chair next to me.

I quickly close my laptop because I don't want him to see that I have been up to nothing. "I'm working on it. I have a couple of ideas floating around in my head. Just been going through a little bit of a mental block. Maybe I've got too much going on in my head."

Quakes perks up. "Oh, I understand that. In my work as an abolitionist I had some truly inspired moments if I do say so myself. I have always had a flair for the dramatic, but I never really went looking for those moments. I just expressed myself or went with the idea once I had it. You cannot force the magic." He has a half grin on his face as if he wants me to ask him about his dramatic flair. He's eating a handful of cashews and the shells are all caught in his beard. It's gross but kind of charming. I can tell he is dying to be indulged, so I play along.

"What are some of the things you did to bring awareness that felt inspired?"

As he hops off his chair a couple of cashew shells hit the floor and he doesn't even acknowledge them. Quakes saunters over to his satchel and I immediately know what he's reaching for. The studio has an almost permanent weed smell thanks to Quakes. Though all of us have partaken, except Harriet.

"I would always try and reason with words first," he says, getting ready to roll something up. "But if I thought I could not get through to people using my powers of communication, I was not afraid to resort to more drastic measures. I was once having a discussion with a slaveholder about how horrible it must feel for a slave to have their children sold, or how it must have felt for Africans whose family members left their homes for the day and never made it back because of the abductions going on along the west coast of Africa."

I was admittedly starting to drift off but Quakes mentioning Africa snaps me back to what he's saying. "Most white people used cognitive dissonance to dislodge themselves from reality. They did not want to look at the truth. That is how they came up with the idea that a Black person is only three-fifths of a person. It allowed them to step away from reality. That way they do not have to treat you like a human, because they have convinced themselves that you are not. That is how they slept at night."

Quakes takes a deep inhale off a large, intimidating-looking blunt and passes it to me. I hesitate, but figuring it could help with my inspiration problem, I take a few pulls.

"But it did not take a lot of looking inside to understand

how false that was," Quakes continues. "There were even rumors that Black people did not feel as much pain as white people because of the amount of suffering we had seen you all go through. When I could not get this slaveholder to put himself in the shoes of a Black parent losing their child with my words, I decided to put him there with my actions. So, I made friends with his family so that his staff would become familiar with me. Because of my stature people never see me as a threat. They often feel sorry for me, until they realize I am capable of everything they are capable of. After I gained access to his home I snuck in one evening and kidnapped his child."

This completely catches me off guard during a heavy pull from the blunt and I have to hack up my lungs for a few seconds. "I'm sorry, what?" I finally manage to choke out.

"The child was with my wife, so I had no concerns for its safety. I watched as he and his family panicked looking for the child for two days. I watched them go through all the stages of grief. After a few days I returned the child. Next time I talked to him about breaking up families in the slave trade he seemed a little more sympathetic."

"I'm still caught up in the whole you kidnapped a baby thing," I say, still astounded.

"I gave her back, do not be so dramatic. Besides, you are missing the point. Kidnapping that child got my point across to the slaveholder. And I was able to make my point to you because I waited for inspiration to strike instead of searching for it."

I don't think I would ever do anything as drastic as that, but I certainly see what he is trying to say. Every once in a while, I forget that I am with a group of people that were all considered fugitives at some point. They are certainly not afraid to break the law.

"Another time I wanted to recruit more Quakers into the abolitionist efforts, so I resorted to a little theatricality. I knew at our core many of us believed in the complete abolition of slavery in theory, but some needed a little more encouragement to join the effort."

I realize that I have opened the floodgates for story time now. Quakes is lounging on a stool, the blunt disappearing in his hand, so I shift in my chair so that I am completely facing him.

"I calmly waited until I felt the Lord speak to me during a meeting, knowing full well what I was going to say when I stood up. I waited until the meeting was almost over and made my voice heard. I stood and said . . . " Quakes then shoots up, ash flying everywhere, as if he's getting ready to address his fellow believers.

"I feel like this congregation has lost its way. We seem to no longer understand what our mission is here. We are to live our lives full of simplicity, peace, integrity, community, equality, and stewardship. I can see that you are all simple. You live off the land to the best of your ability. Many of you even make your own clothes. We are certainly a peaceful people. Maybe even to a fault. We do not desire any amount of chaos or animosity with our fellow man. But where is your integrity? My question to you is when do you do your part to ensure equality? When do you take part to make sure that your fellow man is at least given a chance at equity? I know that the law says that we are not supposed to treat the Negro as an equal, but may I remind you that the law does not dictate who is and is not equal. The Lord dictates that. I think he has made his stance very clear. If you were to see a hungry child on the street, would you not feed them? If you saw that a woman was cold, would you not give her a coat? If you saw a man in pain, would you not get him help? Then it pains me to have to ask you why you have allowed the Negro to suffer as you stand by and do nothing. If you are a silent observer, you are as bad as a slaver himself. We have all seen men bleeding from shackles, children crying from hunger, and women suffering under backbreaking labor that not even a bull of a white man would want to perform, and yet our congregation has done nothing to establish equity with the Negro. I can no longer stand by and watch you all desecrate this Bible in the way you have. If you will not live by these words, then you might as well do away with the book altogether."

He seems so proud of his speech.

"That's when I threw my Bible on the ground, pulled a small dagger from my bag, and plunged it into the Bible. I had hidden some pokeberry juice inside which splashed everywhere like blood, covering me and several of the people sitting near me." Quakes is so excited that he is breathing heavily. "Not everyone appreciated my antics, but I did convert several people that day. I was able to open up about my feelings and change some minds at the same time."

He's so energized that he's worked up a little sweat telling this story, and I must admit it is very entertaining. I don't know how much of it I can relate to myself, though, if I'm being honest.

I appreciate his anecdotes, but they are kind of slowing down my creative process. I don't think it is giving me the inspiration he thinks it is, but I don't have the heart to tell him.

"I needed that, Quakes," I say, even though it is categorically false. Nonetheless, this is such an interesting group of people. "Well, I better get back to work, I think the inspiration is striking." I tell a little white lie so he'll go about his business.

"All right, all right. I get it. Just remember you are allowed to wait for the inspiration to strike." He waddles over to his small chair next to his equipment and starts fiddling with it. He puts on one of the records I recommended to him, David Bowie, *The Rise and Fall of Ziggy Stardust and the Spiders from Mars*. Talk about theatricality.

"Thanks again!" I say a little too loudly across the room. I said it as if he is a football field away.

As I open my laptop again, I start to think about the impact this album could have had on me as a young artist coming up. It's really cool that I get to be part of something so amazing, but the pressure feels insurmountable. I truly wonder if I'll even be able to finish the project. I spend the next ten minutes blankly staring at the screen, not even moving. Harriet must have noticed, because she walks over to me.

"You ain't gotta do everything by yourself, Darnell." She places her small, leathery hand on my shoulder. "I ain't never heard of nobody doing nothing this big by theyself. I spent my whole life relying on people and having people rely on me. The Underground Railroad wasn't nothing but a bunch of folks that thought that freedom was for everybody, not just the ones who already free. If I didn't ask them folks for help, I wouldn't have been able to help nearly as many people. Even the Union Army had to humble theyselves to ask Negroes for help in the war. Course, lot of those

Negroes was happy to have the chance to defend theyselves against a bunch of Southerners. I used to hear them boys talking about what they would do if they ran into they former slave master. They would talk about getting they revenge even though they knew ain't no way they was ever gon' run into they old slave masters, but it gave them something to look forward to. And they relied on one another to make it through the hard times. See! Ain't nobody out here doing nothing by theyselves."

I want to wave Quakes over and show him that this is how you give advice, and no one had to kidnap a baby. But Harriet is right. Maybe I am trying to carry too much of the load myself. Everyone here is an accomplished musician. They've all brought something to this album, something great. I need to lean into the advice and rely on support from the team more. I'm not alone.

"Minty, you're right. I've been doing too much lately. Just slaving away on this project." The moment I said it I regretted it. Everyone in the room stopped what they were doing and looked at me. I can't see them looking at me though, because I am staring at the floor in shame, but I can one hundred percent feel their eyes on me. I'm just panicking because I don't know how to recover from this. I'm so embarrassed, I can't look anyone in the eye. "I am *so* sorry. That's not what I meant. I don't normally talk like that, and—"

Harriet shushes me in the middle of my sentence. "Now hold on. I'm gon' say my piece and be done with it. You ain't never slaved a day in your life. There has never been a day when you woke up as property. There ain't never been a day when you went to sleep at night and had to sleep on your stomach 'cause your back had lashes. There ain't never been a day where you wondered where your family was 'cause they done been sold up the river, and I know you been paid for every bit of work you done in your lifetime. Your ancestors that slaved did that so you wouldn't have to. The folks who ran did that to make damn sure you could walk at your own pace. Now I'm asking you real nice to think about what you say before you say it." She turns her back to me and starts to walk back to her side of the room.

"And hold your head up!" she shouts as she walks away.

After about ten minutes, Moses comes over to my table. "Don't be embarrassed. It's the only thing she sensitive about. She only say it because she don't want nobody to ever have to feel like a slave again. That's her whole life's mission. So her anger ain't got nothing to do with you. It's the system she upset with. I know you smart enough to understand that and not take it personal." He puts his hand on my shoulder and I lean slightly into its weight.

"I know, but I'm still embarrassed. I feel like I can't take that back."

"Well, you can't," he says a bit too quickly. "It's out there. The damage is done. So now instead of acting like the damage never occurred, we can figure out how to repair."

Harriet yells across the room, "You wanna repair, finish this damn album!"

I swear this woman has bionic hearing.

I think that was the motivation I was waiting for. I guess Quakes was right after all. The inspiration came to me. And slapped me across the back of my head. He also may be onto something with his flair for theatricality. I think I found someone to help plan this show.

CHAPTER 15

I TAKE A STEP BACK AND realize that I have actually produced the whole album. Well, *we* did. Odessa was the final piece. She approached me sheepishly a few days ago with a piece of paper in her hand. She had written a song and wanted me to take a look at it, to see if it was any good. It was great. She presented it to the band and we worked on it till it was perfect. Or as close as we could get. Harriet finishes recording her final vocal track and I proudly declare, "That's a wrap on *Queen of the Underground.*"

I feel like I've been in this studio for a year at this point. I don't even know how long it has actually been. It's all starting to feel like a fever dream. As Harriet is taking off her headphones and exiting the booth, Slim suddenly bursts through the door, applauding dramatically. Was he waiting outside the whole time waiting for his cue? Knowing him, probably.

"Congrats, Harriet! And everyone," he says vaguely, gesturing to the Freemans. "And thank you, Darnell. I knew you were the right man for this."

"Yeah, well, it was a team effort."

"Sure. Lemme bend ya ear real quick, Darnell." I have been putting off a one-on-one with him for a while, I guess it's time to hear him out. We head out into the hallway and Slim dismisses his two bodyguards, his agent, and a woman that I swear looks familiar.

"Listen, Slim, whatever you have to say, it's fifteen years too late . . . "

"Nigga, I need a favor," he blurts out.

"Damn, not even an 'I'm sorry'?"

"Nigga, I'm sorry, I need a favor." Considering that he did give me the greatest project of my career, I decide to hear him out. "So the video of me outing you on *Smooth Live* is goin' viral since we announced you was producin' the album."

My heart starts to race and for a minute it feels like I'm back under those hot lights again. "So what do you want me to do about it?"

"Well, I don't really come off that great—"

"No shit."

"And Maxine says I need to make amends."

"Who's Maxine?"

"My publicist."

That's who that woman was, the unbothered girl from the studio all those years ago.

"Your girlfriend?"

"She was never my girlfriend. She just rolled blunts for me and kept up appearances. Though she did work her way through college and get her degree in communications."

"Good for her."

"Right? So I hired her for my publicity team and she's been my publicist for the past decade."

"She must be *very* good."

"She da best. And she got an idea. If you down. Me. You. On Smooth's podcast. Clearin' the air. Showin' they ain't no hard feelin's."

"I don't think so, Slim. I don't have any hard feelings, but you got yourself into this. You and Maxine can get you out." I turn to go back inside the studio when Slim grabs my arm.

"You don't get it, man. This shit ain't just about me, this could sink the whole album. Think of all the work you did. Think about Harriet."

I do think about Harriet. And she is so much bigger, and so much more important, than a fifteen-year-old video, or Slim's dwindling reputation. Harriet would be disappointed in me if I bowed, once again, to this man. And more importantly, *I* would be disappointed in me.

"I'm sorry, Slim. But I have no interest in taking part in a reboot of that interview. I wish you luck holding on to your job." And I disappear into the studio.

"What was that about?" Harriet asks when I return.

I smile and say, "Nothing important. Now, we've got rehearsals in ten."

• • •

Quakes has been invaluable in putting the show together. Instead of a straightforward concert, he's created a mini musical, bringing each song to life. We had a devil of a time getting sets, but Buck, Moses, and Quakes are skilled carpenters and built most of it. Of course, we had to get an electrician in since none of them technically knew what electricity was. Quakes even figured out how to incorporate his pokeberry blood trick into the performance. I think the audience is going to go wild when they see it.

The album was the hard part, but once that was done, the show just kinda came together naturally. Maxine, miracle worker that she is, managed to save Slim's job and in return he left us to do whatever we wanted. The show tells the stories of Harriet's adventures. I wrote down all those stories she told me and together they formed the narrative of the show.

We got cameos from John Brown and Frederick Douglass, too. John Brown is being played by an actor, but the real Frederick Douglass is actually going to be in the show! He lives in Bed-Stuy now.

We're all booked at the Apollo on Juneteenth: "Harriet Tubman and the Freemans present *Queen of the Underground*." I still can't believe we made it.

On the night of the show, I'm a bundle of nerves. I keep peeking out from behind the curtain to see how many people are turning up. There's not an empty seat in the house and we're still an hour to showtime. It seems Black folks will be late to anything except a free Harriet Tubman rap concert. Harriet insisted the concert be free to make sure her people could see her, she said. Still, Slim organized a live stream sponsored by Nike, Amazon, and Starbucks, so the label's making money hand over fist regardless. The whole world must be watching.

Scattered among the crowd are some famous faces who managed to score tickets, despite Harriet's best intentions. Singers, actors, former presidents. I wonder how Harriet would feel seeing Abraham Lincoln's tall, lanky ass here. But I guess no one wants to miss this. The sets have come together nicely. It's a small-scale re-creation of Brodess Farm, not as we saw it, but how Harriet knew it. Most of the set pieces easily move so we can change from a forest, to a Philadelphia street, to a Union Army base camp all within a matter of seconds. Harriet wanted the show to always be moving, to never stop.

On my way backstage, I see a man who looks oddly familiar, the way famous people can look like an old acquaintance until you realize a little too late—oh shit, it's that dude from that show. An older, powerful-looking Black man, tall with white, white hair braided into cornrows. He must see me staring at him so he walks over and asks where the bathroom is. I point him in the right direction only to realize seconds later, a bit too late, that—oh shit, that was Frederick Douglass! The cornrows threw me. A part of me is tempted to go after him, but following strangers into bathrooms is never a good start to a relationship.

The Freemans are all doing their best to cope with their anxiety. Quakes keeps pacing back and forth, chain-smoking blunts, despite being told many times there's no smoking inside. Odessa just keeps putting on more and more makeup and I'm afraid someone is going to have to stop her. Buck just keeps doing push-ups. And Moses is meditating. Only Harriet seems weirdly apart from it all. She's not even drinking any coffee.

I walk up to her and realize that, even after all this time, she still makes me a little nervous. "So this is it. You excited?"

"S'pose."

"Isn't this what you wanted?"

She just shakes her head and gives me a half-hearted smile. It's almost like she is pushing the smile out of the side of her face. Giving me just enough emotion to keep me from being concerned. I don't know how well it's working.

She perks up. "Odessa, baby, that's enough rouge."

"Well," I begin, not sure what's going on with Harriet, "I've got some ideas about our next project. One word: disco. Now, hear me out—"

Suddenly all the Freemans stop and look at me without a word.

"This the hardest part for me," Harriet says, staring into my eyes. "At the end of every journey I know I got to let y'all go." I feel like I've had the wind knocked out of me. "I know I can't walk with you forever, but it don't make it easier to let you walk on your own."

"Harri— Minty, I—"

"I try not to get too attached to folks. That's how I messed around and adopted my daughter. I just couldn't let her go. I grew too attached," she says, cutting me off. I have a feeling this could be the last thing she ever says to me and I don't want to hear it. Not yet. "The truth is, I wouldn't even know what to do if I was walking with you for much longer. I'm still figuring it out myself. White folks got a real head start in this country. We running in a race, but we four hundred years behind. Trying our best to catch up and make something for ourselves. Everything we done made for ourselves they try and tear it down. We make jazz and they tell us it's the devil's music. We decide to give our children French names and they tell us we ghetto. Then they come right behind us, claim it for theyselves, and tell us it's culture, like we never knew. Don't ever give yourself a hard time when we done made it this far. I may have shown you the way on this journey but I didn't carry you. You used your own strength to get here. Whenever I drop somebody off, I wish I could tell them it'll be smooth sailing from here on, but that would be nothing but a lie. Freedom is something you got to keep fighting for every day. They was right when they said freedom don't come free. Especially for people like you and me. So you got to decide what you gon' do with your freedom now. I know what I got to do."

Suddenly everyone is standing around me in a circle. It feels like they're about to join hands and banish me to some other realm. "So . . . y'all are just gonna leave me?" I ask them. They all look down except for Harriet.

"Baby, this was never for me. It was always meant for you," she tells me. "I told you a while ago that I'll do whatever it takes to make sure you get to freedom. You got a lot of people that need to hear this." She pushes a bony finger into my chest. "It's time for you to go tell it on the mountain. You have to make your voice heard so that people who sound like you can come to the mountaintop and sing they own songs. Now you can help somebody else find they voice the way we helped you find yours. You was always capable of that, but somebody made you forget it along the way. It's your turn to lead somebody else to freedom."

I don't know what to say. I finally find my people, a family, and now I have to go out on my own. But, as always, Harriet is right. I've spent the last fifteen years, really, my entire life, hiding, afraid to speak, and more afraid to actually be heard. My eyes well up with tears and I turn my back from everyone to wipe them away because I don't want them to see me cry. That's when Harriet, who I never took for a hugger, wraps me in her arms. Moses, Odessa, Quakes, and even big ole Buck join her and I just stand there, allowing them to love me and allowing myself to love them back. I don't know how long we're in that position, but I hear the announcer call out from nowhere.

"Ladies and gentlemen, Harriet Tubman and the Freemans present, *Queen of the Underground!*"

HARRIET TUBMAN:
LIVE IN CONCERT

THE
LINER
NOTES

QUEEN OF THE UNDERGROUND

WANTED A CHANCE TO WRITE SOME GOOD MUSIC

I MEAN SOME HOOD MUSIC

I'M TALKIING 'BOUT I WISH A MOTHERFUCKER
    WOULD MUSIC

LIBERATE MY PEOPLE THROUGH THE SWAMPS AND THE
    WOODS MUSIC

NEVER WOULD HAVE MADE IT IF I DIDN'T KNOW I COULD
    MUSIC

NO BOOK SMARTS SO THERE WAS VERY LITTLE
    EDUCATION

BUT I MADE IT WITH A LITTLE BIT OF DIVINATION

GOT A CALL TO LIBERATE A GENERATION

SO LET ME SLOW DOWN IF YOU DON'T SEE
    THE CORRELATION

TO FREE MY PEOPLE BECAME MY OBLIGATION

NO JOB NO SKILLS BECAUSE THIS IS MY OCCUPATION

YOU GOTTA USE WHAT YOU GOT SO YOU CAN
    OVERCOME MY SITUATION

OK LADIES, NOW LET'S GET IN FORMATION

YES I'M AMERICAN BUT I'M ALSO BLACK

SO I SPENT MY WHOLE LIFE TRYING TO RECKON
WITH THAT

FROM SLAVE, TO FREE, TO ESCAPING FROM THE
HUNTING GROUND

GOT NICKNAMED MOSES, QUEEN OF
THE UNDERGROUND RAILROAD

NOT A CHANCE IN HELL I CAN FAIL ROAD

LIBERATE MY PEOPLE AND GET FREE BY THE BOATLOAD

SO WADE IN THE WATER 'CAUSE I GUARANTEE IT'S
GOING DOWN

'CAUSE YOU'RE HARRIET, QUEEN OF
THE UNDERGROUND

WE'RE IN THE HOME OF THE BRAVE AND THE LAND OF
THE FREE

SO I HAVE TO FIGURE OUT WHAT FREEDOM REALLY
MEANS TO ME

I HAVE THE RIGHT TO DEATH OR I HAVE THE RIGHT
TO LIBERTY

AND IT'S ONE OR THE OTHER THERE'S NO ROOM
FOR FLEXIBILITY

SLAVERY OUR COUNTRY'S FIRST MASS INCARCERATION

AND I KNOW THAT THAT'S A HEAVY ALLIGATION

ABOLITION NOW, I MEAN COMPLETE ANNIHILATION

BUT BLACKS WILL BE FREE AND IT IS NOT UP

    FOR NEGOTIATION.

THIS NATION IS SICK AND KNOWLEDGE IS THE ANTIDOTE

BUT NOT JUST FOR MEN GIVE SUFFRAGETTES THE RIGHT

    TO VOTE

SEE THAT BAND ALL DRESSED IN WHITE

I SAID THAT MUST BE THE BAND OF THE ISRAELITES

SEE THAT BAND ALL DRESSED IN RED

THAT MUST BE THE BAND THAT MOSES LED

BUT DO YOU SEE THAT BAND ALL DRESSED IN BROWN

THAT'S THE BAND OF MOSES, QUEEN OF THE

    UNDERGROUND

SO MEET ME AT THE WATER 'CAUSE I GUARANTEE IT'S

    GOING DOWN

'CAUSE YOU'RE HARRIET, QUEEN OF THE UNDERGROUND

THE MAINSTREAM MAY KNOW ABOUT ME NOW

BUT I WILL ALWAYS BE QUEEN OF THE UNDERGROUND.

NOW I SEE

AS SHE STAND IN THE DOORWAY HUFFIN' AND SWEATIN'
REALIZING SHE'S FIERCE BECAUSE HER BABY HAD
    BEEN THREATENED
I SEE A WOMAN AT HER WITS' END
AND SHE WOULD NOT BEND
AND FOR THE FIRST TIME THIS WAS SOMETHING I COULD
    COMPREHEND
DOING WHAT SHE HAD TO DO SO SHE COULD SAVE
    HER FAMILY
STARING AT A MAN WITHOUT A SINGLE BIT OF APATHY
SUCH A THIN LINE BETWEEN THE BAD AND THE
    GOOD GUYS
I CAN SEE TEARS BUT NO FEAR IN MY MOMMA'S EYES
THE PLAN TO INTIMIDATE HAD BACKFIRED
I DON'T THINK THEY EVEN UNDERSTAND
    WHAT TRANSPIRED
MY MOMMA UNDERSTAND WHAT SHE INSPIRED
WHEN YOU'RE JUST SICK AND TIRED OF BEING SICK AND
    TIRED

THAT'S WHEN I REALIZED YOU CAN BE WHAT YOU
    WANNA BE

NOTHING COMES FOR FREE IN THIS LIFE, THAT'S
    A GUARANTEE.

FIGHT FOR THE RIGHTS YOU WANT 'CAUSE NO BODY IS A
    NOBODY

AND THAT'S THE DAY I DECIDED I WANNA BE FREE

NOW I SEE THIS AIN'T THE LIFE I'M SUPPOSED TO
    BE LIVING

DESPITE THE HAND I WAS GIVEN

THIS AIN'T THE GRAVE I'M DIGGING.

NOW I SEE THAT I CAN REACH BEYOND WHAT I
    CAN SEE

AND I DESERVE TO BE FREE

AND THAT IT'S UP TO ME

NOW I SEE EVEN IF YOU WERE BORN A SLAVE

YOU GET A CHANCE TO BE BRAVE

ESCAPE AN EARLY GRAVE

NOW I SEE I GOTTA LEAVE THIS BEHIND IF I WANNA
    BE ME

I DIDN'T SEE IT, BUT NOW I SEE, NOW I SEE

SO I REALLY HAD TO CHANGE THE WAY I THINK,

HAD TO CHANGE THE WAY I AM

UNDO MY MIND, GET OUT THE KINKS, LOOK AT MY LIFE
    AND REEXAM

SEE MYSELF AS AN EQUAL AND NOT A PIECE OF LAND

ASK GOD TO HAVE HIS WAY WITH ME SO I
    CAN UNDERSTAND

SO CHANGE ME GOD

R:

UNDO ME, FIX ME.

HARRIET:

HELP ME FIND A WAY TO MAKE IT

R:

OUT OF THE DIXIE.

HARRIET:

I DON'T WANNA WAIT

R:

PLEASE HELP ME DO IT QUICKLY

DON'T WANNA WAIT FOR FREEDOM TILL I'M FORTY-FIVE
    OR FIFTY

R:

THEY STRIP US OF OUR DIGNITY

AND PUT US UP FOR AUCTION

KEEPING US IN CHAINS SO WE THINK WE DON'T HAVE
    NO OPTIONS
I NEED AMAZING GRACE. HOW SWEET THE SOUND?
DON'T WANNA TURN THIS PLACE INTO MY
    BURIAL GROUND
I ONCE WAS LOST, BUT NOW I'M FOUND
GOTTA PUT A PLAN IN ACTION, I'M NOT FUCK-
    ING AROUND
YOU SEE I ONCE WAS BLIND, BUT NOW I SEE
I HAD TO GET THIE VEIL OFF MY EYE EVENTUALLY SO I
    COULD SEE

ACKNOWLEDGMENTS

I AM MOST THANKFUL FOR THE dedication and support of so many people who helped me bring Harriet's story to life in a new light. Without them, none of this would be possible.

To my agent, Tom Flannery—thank you for believing in this very special project and for being the best literary champion I could have asked for.

To my editor, James Melia—I cannot think of a better person to entrust this story with, and I am incredibly grateful for your unwavering enthusiasm at every turn.

And to the entire team at Gallery Books for their strong belief in my talent and ability: Jennifer Bergstrom, Aimee Bell, Matt Attanasio, Sally Marvin, Sophie Normil, Sydney Morris, Caroline Pallotta, Alysha Bullock, and Hope Herr-Cardillo.

To my creative confidant, Lester Fabian Brathwaite, I truly appreciate your input, support, and for really taking the time to understand my voice and vision.

To my assistant, Kennedy Warner—I truly could not have made it this far without you, thank you for keeping me one step ahead, and for your unfaltering kindness while doing so.

To my Shore Fire Media team—thank you for always being in my corner and for cheering me on as this came so wonderfully to fruition.

And because it always takes a village, thank you to my Producer Entertainment Group family, especially De'Vaughn Williams, Jacob Slane, and David Carpentier, for always keeping my best interests in mind and heart. And my trusty focus group, you know who you are—thank you for easing my mind, and for your honesty, time, and enthusiasm as I put the final touches on this book.